Burned on Sunday: A Colorado Reckoning Western

K Wendt

Distributed by Bublish, Inc.

Cover design by Bublish, Inc.

Paperback ISBN: 978-1-950282-53-1

eBook ISBN: 978-1-950282-69-2

Burned on Sunday

Chapter One

"For the sinner is condemned to hell!"

Pastor Tom's words echoed through the church as he said again, "The sinner is condemned to hell—eternal damnation for his sins. By lusting after another man's wife, he does not know God."

The pastor's face reddened increasingly with fury on each word, and his finger pointed to the sinful congregation before him, condemning all. He couldn't condemn Lucy, though, without turning the finger on himself. Pastor Tom Moore was a hypocrite.

Lusting after a woman was only considered wrong if done outside the saloon walls and everyone in town, or at least the male population, knew it. In the town's eyes, the saloon women were a bad habit, just like the beer at the bar the soiled doves called home.

It was well-known that most every man in town went to the saloon to drink. What people weren't sure about was which men climbed the stairs into the saloon girls' beds.

Lucy sat in the back pew every Sunday. She knew God was probably unhappy with her career choice, but in her defense, she was just a hurdy-gurdy girl. Matthew made sure dancing with the men was all she did, outside of helping Ms. Betty with chores, after the incident with Sam.

When Lucy had arrived in Rock Springs, she hadn't even been able to come up with money for a meal. She thought she had planned everything out so well when she left her home back in the east, but as her Aunt Judy always had a way of pointing out, she was too young and naïve to account for bad weather days and wagon wheels breaking traversing the hard, dry ground.

As an educated woman of sixteen years of age, Lucy could have taught the town's children, but that position was filled by a woman in her thirties, still awaiting her Prince Charming's arrival, and she had grown to love the children.

Lucy had looked at several positions. If she had stayed with her aunt as she was supposed to, Lucy would have been a governess to the children of the bank president, but Lucy didn't want that job. Nor did she want to be married off to some rich family, which had been the goal set out for her by the death of her father and the social standing of her mother. To her dismay, the only job open when she came to town was that of a dancing girl. The saloon had lost a girl when she married an out of town man and moved off with him.

The saloon keeper provided room and meals, cooked by Ms. Betty, who looked after all the girls. She cared for them when they were sick and wouldn't let a man touch them when their "sister" visited.

Lucy had never been with a man, and the idea of it really scared her. Lucky for her, the girls had to work their way up to entertaining men behind closed doors. And Lucy's homely looks gave her an advantage, as far as she was concerned, because it kept the men from wanting anything more than dancing with her.

Tom was a hypocrite, shaking his finger at everyone. Lucy knew his secret—where he spent the late hours of the night three days of the week. Yet, because a man and a married woman lusted after each other outside of the saloon, it was a sin, and it was Pastor Tom's job to remind the congregation how wrong it was.

Lucy felt sorry for the woman caught in the affair. She had received the harshest punishment by being forced to stay in her loveless marriage.

Lucy knew what a jerk her best friend's husband was firsthand. She had seen the bruises Mark had left on Melissa's back, and they were there before she was caught in the affair. Mark was ten years older than Melissa, and he'd only married her because he needed a new mom for his recently orphaned children. Melissa had been a lot like Lucy when she'd arrived—penniless and hungry—so she'd agreed to marry Mark and raise his kids.

Until he married Melissa, Mark was a regular in the saloon who found his way up the stairs. He still came in occasionally, but he stayed away from Lucy because he knew she and Melissa were friends.

Melissa had admitted to Lucy that she had hoped he would love her, but instead, she'd become a servant. The children expected motherly duties performed for them, and Mark expected his husbandly desires to be taken care of. They ran her until she couldn't stand up.

Mark had a farmhand named Ted, who was six feet tall and had brown hair and eyes. His sculpted muscles showed off his hard work, and Melissa became attracted to him because he was friendly to her and conversation was something missing in her life. It didn't take long for the attraction between them to grow.

Mark caught them three months into the affair when he came home early from town. They were in the barn, half-undressed, when they heard him from the barn door yelling for them to come out. Ted had to leave town and promise never to come back, and Melissa had to promise to stay or Mark would kill Ted. After Ted left, Mark beat her so badly she couldn't move for a week.

Mark was a man of high standing in the community with his keen business sense, productive farm, and was consider one of the big men in town. He had a lot of power, so when word got out that his wife was sleeping with another man, the town sympathized with him and shunned Melissa.

Today was Melissa's first day back in church. People stared at her with pure evil in their eyes, blind to the freshly bruised eye she was trying so hard to hide.

Pastor Tom knew Melissa would be there today, and he knew the townspeople would expect something dramatic. That's why he was in such a condemning mood, up there getting all hot in the face, pointing and yelling. But Lucy knew better, and if he didn't get off her friend's back, she was going to make sure his sins were uncovered as well.

As Lucy scanned the room, she saw many hypocrites' faces. This town was a farce. Everything here was built on lies, and it was time the walls came tumbling down.

❧

Chapter Two

Matthew Clarkson was setting up the bar for the after-church crowd when Lucy walked into the saloon after the Sunday "morning show" was done.

Matthew was in his mid-fifties and balding on the top of his head. Other than Ms. Betty, he was the only source of protection for all the girls. On the outside, he was gruff and hard to know, but inside, he was all mush.

"Betty has lunch waiting in the kitchen. The way I hear it, Pastor Tom was really laying it on thick today. Should mean a big crowd for us," Matthew said.

Lucy smiled while inwardly rolling her eyes. She never said she liked her job but it got her by.

"I'll go help Ms. Betty set the table," she said, heading toward the kitchen when she noticed a man passed out at a table in the corner. Lucy asked. "I thought you kicked everyone out last night."

"I did. I found him when I came in this morning. He wouldn't wake up, so I'm letting him sleep it off a little longer," Matthew explained.

"Interesting. You made sure he isn't dead, right?" she asked.

"I'm not dead. I rode all night on my horse and just needed a place to rest." The stranger stood up, stretched, took some money from his pocket, and tossed it on the table. "That's for the use of the chair and table. I'll be on my way," he told them.

The stranger was a tall, handsome creation of a man with brown hair and brown eyes that shone under the hat he had just placed on his head.

"Well, why don't you eat before you go?" Matthew asked. "Lucy, show him to the kitchen. Tell Betty I said it was okay for him to eat lunch with us."

"Yes, sir," she said to Matthew. "Follow me," Lucy told the stranger.

In the two years Lucy had been there, all the men she had seen or danced with had disgusted her, but there was something about this man—something enticing, something drinkable.

Lucy opened the kitchen door and held it so the man behind her could enter. She tried hard to be nonchalant. Ms. Betty's back was to them as she stirred something delicious-smelling on the stove.

"Ms. Betty, this gentleman is joining us for lunch. Matthew said it was okay."

Betty turned and looked at her strangely. "Lucy, what's wrong, girl? You look flushed," she said.

Lucy put her hand to her cheek. "I'm fine. Guess I got hot walking from the church."

"Well, take it easy for a bit, just in case," Ms. Betty said, looking at the man. "What's your name, stranger?"

"Henry."

"A perfect name for such a handsome man," Lucy thought. She noticed that his facial features seemed deep and perfectly shadowed by hours in the sun. She felt her cheeks flush again and quickly turned away to start setting the table.

"Nice to meet you, Henry. Are you staying with us long?" Ms. Betty asked.

"No, just passing through," Henry answered.

"Well, I'll get your belly good and full and you can be on your way, if you like," Ms. Betty said.

"Thank you," Henry replied, pulling out a chair near Lucy and removing his hat. His hair was full and thick and his skin was tanned from long rides on horseback.

&

"Oh my God! Did you see how red Pastor Tom's face got during his sermon?" Catherine said.

"Adultery is sin. Honestly, how are we supposed to make a living if none of the men want someone different than their wives every now and then?" Lauren replied.

"Especially Mark. Melissa is so plain."

Catherine and Lauren opened the kitchen door and looked from Ms. Betty to Henry.

"Oops!" Catherine said. "Ms. Betty, who's this handsome man?"

"Who has the pleasure of his company today? Surely not Lucy," Lauren said, giving Lucy a disapproving look.

"I'm not staying. Just passing through," Henry told them.

"Well, that's a shame," Lauren said, feigning disappointment.

"Catherine, go get the other girls. Lunch is ready, and I want to serve it while it's hot so our guest can be on his way," Ms. Betty said.

"Yes, ma'am."

Lauren sat down next to Henry and eyed him head to toe. "Why the hurry just to pass through? Don't you like our little town?" she asked.

"Lauren, don't be so rude," Ms. Betty scolded, placing the last platter on the table.

Matthew and all the other girls came in and took their places. Once everyone was seated, he said grace, thanking God for the food on the table and asking for protection for the guest and for the girls as they did their jobs.

It might have seemed hypocritical for Matthew to pray for what those in the saloon did for a living, but Matthew and Betty treated all the girls like family. They believed in God and so did some of the girls, and it was nice to believe that maybe God would watch over the sinners.

There was none of the usual town gossip or customer chatter at lunch that day. The table was unusually quiet as all the females except Ms. Betty took a good look at the the handsome stranger.

Henry didn't look up from his plate until the last bite. He put his fork down, cleaned his hands and face with his napkin, pushed his chair out, and grabbed his hat as he got up.

"Thank you for the meal. I'd better be on my way," Henry said, looking at Lucy briefly, and then shifting his gaze to Ms. Betty. "That was the best meal I've had in a while."

"Are you sure you have to rush off?" Ms. Betty asked out of politeness. She knew his hanging around wouldn't be good for the girls.

"Yes, ma'am. I have business I have to tend to. Thanks for sharing your meal." He tipped his hat, met Lucy's gaze briefly again, and was gone.

"Ooh, a mystery man," said Sarah. "Wonder what his business is."

"That's none of our concern," Ms. Betty said, trying to hide her relief that the stranger had left. She didn't like men just popping in outside of business hours, and there was something about this stranger she didn't like—something familiar that made her leery of him.

&

Lucy went to bed that night dreaming about Henry. She had spent the afternoon comparing her customers to him. While some of the men were tall and others had dark eyes, none of them seemed to have the twinkle that was in Henry's eyes. The rest of his body wasn't bad either, but his eyes drew her in. Henry was a mystery—one that wouldn't be solved since he had left town.

Lucy sighed as she got up the next day. She had a plan that needed to be set into motion. She just needed to figure out the best place to start. The people in this town were going to wish they'd never made an example of Melissa.

&

Chapter Three

Henry woke to the smell of coffee brewing. He rolled onto his side and could see Beth at the kitchen stove just beyond the bedroom door. He took in her figure, noting her nice, hourglass shape—perfect for holding, caressing, and being intimate. Her long blond hair was down and danced on her back as she moved. Rolling onto his back, Henry took a deep breath.

"What am I doing here?" he wondered. "This is crazy. It's not okay to be here like this, having to do his brother's work. Beth wasn't his wife, she was Sam's wife. The only girl Henry needed to take care of was Charlette and he couldn't wait to get back home to her."

"Henry, you need to get moving if you want breakfast," Beth said as she went outside to call her six-year-old son, Sammy.

Henry got out of bed and got dressed.

"Morning, Uncle Henry."

"Good morning, Sammy." Henry took a seat at the table with Beth and Sammy. The empty chair was very noticeable this morning. "Any word from Sam?"

"No, not since the last letter I sent you," Beth said.

"What letter?" Sammy asked. "Did we hear from Pa?"

"No, this is business stuff, son," Beth told him. "That's why Uncle Henry is here—so he can help with a few things while your dad is away."

"Right," Henry thought. "I'm here to help Beth fix the dilapidated place my brother left her in. She can do better than Sam. What kind of man leaves his wife to raise his child alone while he travels and tries to find riches?"

The last letter Sam had sent stated clearly that he had no intention of coming home. The money was good in Nevada, and there were rumors of gold mines. Sam had said the landscape there was beautiful and that he would send money to Beth soon.

"He didn't say anything about having his wife and son join him, though," Henry thought. "Sam doesn't understand that a family needs the man at home, and he's a fool for not wanting to be with Beth all the time. She's beautiful and tenderhearted. She deserves the love of a man willing to sacrifice everything for her." Pushing his thoughts aside, Henry said, "After breakfast, let's go see what all needs to be done around here. We'll make a supply list and go to town tomorrow." Henry told Sammy.

"Town! Oh boy!" Sammy squealed.

❧

Lucy decided that the first step of her plan had to take place at Melissa's house, so she headed out to pay her a visit. Lucy had borrowed Ms. Betty's horse, Rose, whom she decided to hitch up in the barn after watching Mark's five hellions terrorizing the family dog with sticks as she rode up.

"I didn't know you were planning to come out here this week."

Lucy turned toward Melissa's voice. The look on her face said she wasn't thrilled to see her.

"I just felt like riding out and talking," Lucy said.

Melissa's face didn't change.

"Is that okay?" Lucy asked.

Melissa tried to smile. "Sure it is. Come on into the house."

Lucy followed Melissa to the house, noticing a slight limp in her walk that wasn't there before. Once they were seated inside, Lucy asked her about it.

"Limp? I'm not limping."

"Come on, Melissa. I could see it clear as day as we walked in here from the barn. What happened?"

"I tripped."

"Really?"

"Yes, really. I tripped in the barn earlier."

Lucy didn't believe her. She knew better but couldn't push her now. "What did you think about the sermon yesterday?" Lucy asked.

Melissa looked at her for a bit before answering. "Pastor Tom is right. Adultery is a sin."

"And?"

"And? That's it. He's right. I'm a sinner, and I have to pay my consequences."

"Do you really believe that?"

"It's in the Bible, Lucy. Why wouldn't I believe it?"

"I'm not disputing what the Bible says. I'm asking if you believe what Pastor Tom said."

"I don't understand. He stated what the Bible says. He was just reminding me...us...the congregation what the Bible says."

"Do you like Pastor Tom?"

"Lucy, are you all right? That's a strange question!"

"How? I just asked if you like him."

"Of course, I like him. He's our pastor. It would be sacrilegious not to."

Lucy sat silently for a minute, thinking about the conversation they were having. "Melissa isn't going to understand," she thought. "I'm going to have to do things on my own."

"Lucy," Melissa said, snapping her out of her thoughts. "Lucy, what is it? Why do you want to know if I like Pastor Tom?"

"It's nothing, Melissa. I'm just making conversation. How are you doing? And tell me the truth."

Henry and Sammy spent the morning going around the place, making a list of supplies.

"I can't wait to go to town," Sammy kept saying all through the morning.

When Beth called them in for lunch, Henry asked how close town was.

"You should know. You went right through it coming here," she answered.

"The last town I passed is a good fifteen miles away," Henry said.

"Yes, Rock Springs."

"Why would Sam move you out here so far from town?"

"He was sure this was prime land for raising cattle. After a few years here, though, he couldn't stand it and decided to go west."

Henry shook his head and went outside. He needed air. He was disgusted with his brother. Sam had left Beth and Sammy stranded with practically everything on their property broken. "I'll see if the town has a way to send a telegram tomorrow," Henry thought.

Chapter Four

Sammy was chatty on the ride into town. He told Henry all about the animals they had and about his "secret places" on the property.

"Sammy, why don't you go on into the mercantile and pick out some candy. I'll be along in a minute," Henry said when they got into town. He stayed in the wagon, taking the envelope that held the message he wanted to send to his brother from his pocket, while his nephew got down.

"You gonna tell my Pa he's no good for nothin'?" Sammy asked.

Henry was shocked. "Why would I do that?"

"Because he is."

Henry was baffled by Sammy's honesty. "Uh...well...I'll meet you inside in just a bit."

Fifteen minutes later, Henry could hear Sammy's voice carrying to the mercantile entrance as he walked in.

"So you see, Miss, that's why molasses is better. It's the flavor."

"Oh, I see," the girl standing next to him said.

"Sammy," Henry called as he walked toward him, "I hope you aren't bothering anyone."

"Oh, he's fine. He's been entertaining me with his thoughts on the different candies."

Henry looked at the girl speaking to him, only she wasn't a girl. She was one of the saloon girls he had shared a meal with two days ago.

"Hello. Still not feeling well?" Henry asked, seeing Lucy's cheeks were red like they had been that day.

She put her hands up to her cheeks. "H-hello. Oh, no, I'm fine. I...uh...I need to get back to work." Lucy rushed past Henry, forgetting her package on the counter.

"Lucy," Mr. DeWitt called.

Henry grabbed the bag and went after her. "Lucy. Hey, Lucy," he called out. "You forgot your package."

Lucy stopped just down the walk, where he caught up with her. "Thank you. How did you know my name?" she asked.

"The merchant said it as he tried to catch you before you left."

"Oh, well, thanks again," she said as she turned to go.

"My name is Henry," he reminded her. He could see the red on Lucy's cheeks had darkened and could see she was nervous.

"Nice to meet you, Henry. I'm Lucy, as you know. Staying in town longer this time?"

"No, I'm not staying at all. My brother's place is about fifteen miles out. My nephew and I just came to town for a few things."

"Oh, who's your brother? Maybe I know the family."

"Sam Bower. I doubt you know him though." Henry tried to hide the agitation in his voice.

"Thank you for getting my package to me. Have a good day," Lucy said and walked off. Henry watched her go, wondering what had gone wrong just then.

❧

Lucy's cheeks burned with anger. "I know who Sam Bower is all right!" she thought. "Henry talks like his brother wouldn't do business in a saloon, but it was Sam's favorite place." The whole town knew that, but Lucy gathered that Henry expected better from his brother. "Hypocrites!" she said to herself. "Just like this town, he judged me for what I did and not for who I am."

Lucy was agitated the rest of the day. Try as she might, she couldn't get Henry and his words out of her head. After supper, she sat down at the small desk in her room to work on her plan. She had two targets in mind: Pastor Tom and Mark.

She wanted Mark to pay for all the things he'd done to Melissa, but Pastor Tom was more personal. She didn't think a man who acted innocent on Sunday but sinned during the week should be sending fire and brimstone down on her.

Lucy knew her job was disgraceful in the eyes of many, but it put food in her stomach. She didn't need any added guilt, and she had a pretty good idea how she wanted to expose the town's beloved pastor. Mark would be harder to deal with because of his temper, and she had to make sure whatever was done wouldn't be taken out on Melissa.

Once Lucy felt good about her plan, she burned the paper over the candle on her desk. Sins of others would be exposed and she didn't want anyone knowing she was the one behind what was going to happen.

❧

Henry couldn't shake the image of Lucy as he worked. She was a pretty woman with raven-colored hair, sky-blue eyes, and a soft, ivory complexion. He wondered why she worked in a saloon. It didn't seem to fit her.

Lost in his daydreams, Henry was oblivious to his surroundings. Sammy had to call out to him a couple of times to get his attention. "I have to get Lucy out of my head," Henry thought. "I'm not staying here long and need to focus on the job I need to do."

❧

Chapter Five

The next morning, Lucy visited Mrs. Martha DeWitt to set her plan in motion. She was on the church committee and carried a lot of weight, though she never voiced her opinion publicly. Her husband was a mouse of a man who did her bidding, and everyone knew it.

Beatrice, the maid, answered the DeWitts' door. "How can I help you?" she asked.

"I'd like to speak with Mrs. DeWitt, please."

"Whom shall I say is asking for her?"

"Lucy, from the saloon. I wanted to talk to her about some church stuff."

"Just a minute, please."

Beatrice left Lucy on the front stoop to tell Mrs. DeWitt of her arrival. A few minutes later, Beatrice opened the door again, led Lucy into a large sitting room, and pointed to a straight-backed, red-upholstered chair. Lucy took the assigned seat and waited for Mrs. DeWitt, who entered shortly thereafter, all prim and proper, wearing the latest fashion in women's dresses.

She looked down at Lucy. "What can I do for you?" she asked.

"Well, Mrs. DeWitt, I've been thinking as of late, and I would like to leave the saloon."

Mrs. DeWitt's ears perked up. "What does this have to do with me?" she asked.

"I want to change my standing in the community. I know people look down on me."

"Again, what does this have to do with me?" Mrs. DeWitt asked.

"You weren't in my position when I came here hungry."

"Why are you telling me this?"

"I know in order to change my ways, I have to change my activities and those I'm around. You know how this town is. I'm forever marked as a soiled dove, a painted lady, or whatever term you prefer to use, but I can't leave. I don't have the means to do so."

"Are you asking for money?"

"No, ma'am. I'm asking for help in a different way. See, I figure with a reference like yours, I could get a job at the mercantile."

"And why would I want to give you a reference?" Lucy heard the annoyance in Mrs. DeWitt's voice. "I don't really know anything about you, and I don't associate with your kind of people."

"Yes, ma'am. I know that, but your husband does associate with my kind." Lucy watched the shock wash over Mrs. DeWitt's face.

"My husband only goes to the saloon to drink a beer and play cards. He told me so, and he wouldn't lie to me."

"Well, sure, he plays cards sometimes, Mrs. DeWitt, if you want to be that naïve—when a certain one of us isn't available for him to spend time with."

Mrs. DeWitt's face was crimson red. "How dare you! You're a lying little..."

"Believe what you want, but I have nothing to lose by telling you all this." Lucy stood up to leave. "I'm not trying to get anything from you other than a good word so I can clean up my life. If you won't help me, I'll find someone who will. There are plenty of wives in this town who don't want everyone knowing exactly what their husbands do in the saloon. But there is only one husband that has fathered a child in one of those beds."

Lucy, pleased with herself, left Mrs. DeWitt staring after her as walked back to the saloon. She had been nervous when she first knocked on the DeWitts' door but had gained confidence as she exposed Mr. DeWitt's secret.

The town's two-faced way was starting to get to Lucy. People, especially other women, looked at her and the saloon girls with disgust in their eyes. They chided the girls for the way they chose to live and were unwilling to admit their husbands' parts in the earning the girls made. Nobody in town except for Ms. Betty really knew anything about Lucy. She had shared a little bit with her once about the dreams she had of being an artist. Lucy still spent most early evening hours drawing.

When she had first arrived in Rock Springs, she spent a few days drawing her entire journey from memory. Her sketches of the town and its people are hidden in the bureau in her room. She never shared them with anyone because no one saw her as anything more than a dancing girl. She didn't know anyone—not even Melissa—she felt would appreciate her artistic ability. She thought about all the townspeople as she sat down at the desk in her room later that day. As she pulled out paper and some pencils, she thought about how Henry had looked at her earlier. She wished he viewed her differently than the others here did. Tears stung her eyes as she began to draw his features.

❦

Chapter Six

"Ah hell," Henry said, throwing a broken piece of wood aside. "The least Sam could have done was get good quality lumber for the barn," Henry thought kicking at the pile of rotted wood. "How did Sam ever expect Beth to keep it up without help?"

Unfortunately, Henry was just beginning to learn how bad off his sister-in-law and nephew were. They were broke and only had what they could grow or raise to eat, and Beth had to figure out how to make do with what they had.

Henry was glad he'd thought to bring some money with him, but he was going to have to see if he could trade for a few things. The lumber they had wouldn't suffice to patch up the barn, so he carried it to the pile for the wood-burning stove. Tomorrow, once he was back from town, he would cut the wood into smaller pieces for Beth to use.

"Why can't I go with ya, Uncle Henry?" Sammy asked.

Henry knelt down to Sammy's level. "I don't intend to be long. Besides, someone has to help your mama pick the vegetables from the garden."

Sammy's brow furrowed.

"You can go next time." Henry stood up and ruffled his nephew's blond hair. "I'll see you two in a while."

Henry climbed into the wagon and waved as Sammy watched him go. He felt bad for telling Sammy he couldn't go, but Henry needed the ride to clear his head and calm himself down. He wondered when his brother would receive the telegram he had sent. Then his thoughts drifted to Lucy.

"She sure is pretty," he thought. "Wonder what caused her mood to change so fast the other day?" He laughed. "Lucy must have a lot of spirit in her—like a wild mustang. Wonder if she has a beau?" he thought, then caught himself and shook it away. He needed to focus on helping Beth and Sammy. Besides, Charlotte was waiting for him back home.

Charlotte was Henry's whole world. He had reluctantly left her with his parents while he was away, and he missed her dearly. She had cried when he left, but Henry knew she would just be underfoot if he brought her along.

At a year old, she was just starting to walk. Henry laughed, realizing "run" was more like it. She had been a good baby, especially with him becoming a widower the night of her birth. Henry's wife, Molly, was redheaded, green-eyed, and freckled head to toe. She was the most beautiful woman Henry had ever known, and Charlotte looked just like her.

Henry decided to send a telegram to his little girl while he was in town. He wanted to know how she was doing. He also sent another telegram to Sam, and he would send as many as he had to, as often as he could, to get his brother to see what he had left behind.

❧

Mrs. DeWitt sent a note to Lucy. The note read, "After much prayer, I feel we should discuss things further."

Lucy wondered what exactly Mrs. DeWitt had prayed about, but it didn't matter. Lucy's plan was slowly coming alive. She hurriedly touched up her hair and rushed out of the saloon.

Once on the boardwalk, Lucy slowed down and took a breath. She needed to be in control of how things progressed, and she also needed the butterflies in her stomach to go away.

As Lucy sat down on Mrs. DeWitt's settee, she wondered what the woman before her was going to say. Lucy studied Mrs. DeWitt's features as the lady of the house took her time to speak. She looked like she hadn't been sleeping well and didn't seem pleased to see Lucy again.

Mrs. DeWitt cleared her throat. "Before we discuss the matter you brought before me the other day, I'd like for a few things to be made clear," she said.

"Okay."

"The last time you were here, you said you wanted to repent of your ways and make a better life for yourself. Is that correct?"

"Yes."

"And fearing I wouldn't help you," Mrs. DeWitt continued, "you threatened me with knowledge about my husband."

"Yes," Lucy replied, trying to remain strong and unsure of where the conversation was headed.

"You claim that my husband has an illegitimate child, correct?"

"Yes."

"How can you be so sure that the child you speak of belongs to my husband?"

Lucy took a deep breath. "Mrs. DeWitt, the child, a young boy, is the spitting image of your husband. Mr. DeWitt frequents the saloon, and there is only one girl there he prefers the company of."

"I'm still not convinced the child you speak of was fathered by my husband."

"He brings a piece of candy to the boy every time he comes to the saloon, Mrs. DeWitt," Lucy interrupted. "Even Mr. DeWitt can't deny the boy is his." Lucy could see red rising up Mrs. DeWitt's neck.

"Show me the child," Mrs. DeWitt said.

"I'm afraid I can't do that."

"Why not?" Mrs. DeWitt asked.

"He's never alone. Everyone is very protective of him," Lucy said.

"Rubbish," Mrs. DeWitt huffed. "You're lying. There isn't a child."

"No, ma'am. I'm not lying," Lucy said. "Ms. Betty sometimes takes him to the mercantile with her. You can see him that way. She usually goes every Thursday."

"Thursday? That's tomorrow. How can you be sure she'll have the boy with her?" Mrs. DeWitt asked.

"I can't. It'll depend on if his mom is busy," Lucy answered.

"I'm not discussing anything further with you until I see the boy."

"That's fine, but in the meantime, be thinking about how you can help me get a job in the mercantile." Lucy smiled as she let herself out.

❧

Lucy knew that if Mrs. DeWitt thought about it long enough, she would realize she's already seen the child. Ms. Betty kept Wyatt with her pretty much all the time.

Lucy thought about Lauren, the boy's beautiful mother, who constantly teased her for her homely looks. Lauren even teased Lucy for only being one of the dancing girls, but that never really bothered her.

Lucy's job had made her hate herself, and she was thankful for the day Ms. Betty and Matthew decided she could help more with the chores instead of entertaining men, although she still had to dance with the men in the evenings if there was a big crowd.

The men all seemed to prefer the more experienced girls anyway, though, and Lucy felt like they all purposely stayed away from her after what happened, which didn't bother her one bit.

❧

Chapter Seven

Lucy went to the back of the saloon and entered through the kitchen. Ms. Betty was working on that night's stew, and Wyatt was at the table enjoying freshly baked sugar cookies.

"Mmm. Those sure do look good," Lucy said.

Wyatt smiled and wrapped his hand around the cookies in front of him. "Can't have 'em. They're all mine," he said with a mouthful.

Lucy laughed, walked over to the counter, and took a cookie from the plate. "Can I help with anything, Ms. Betty?" Lucy asked.

Henry had seen Lucy walk around to the back of the saloon. He wondered if that was where she was going and why. He hoped she wasn't that type of girl.

He slumped forward as he went into the telegram office to see if Sam had responded. "Too many girls find their way to the saloons," he thought. He prayed his Charlotte never would.

After sending his two telegrams, Henry went to pick up a few supplies. He kept looking toward the saloon to see if she was one those girls. For some reason, he had to know.

❦

Lucy dropped the dry clothes into the basket at her feet. She was deliberately taking her time removing the clothes from the line. The sun felt great on her face, and she wanted to enjoy its warmth.

She took the last item off the line and carried the basket inside, placing it on a chair just inside the door. "I'll iron for you after supper," she told Ms. Betty.

"That'll be fine," Ms. Betty said. "Why don't you set the table? Supper isn't too far away."

"Yes, ma'am," Lucy replied. "Would you like to help me, Wyatt?"

Wyatt's eyes lit up as he smiled. He loved "helping" around the saloon.

Lucy put stacks of plates on the table. Together, she and Wyatt put them in their proper places, one dish at a time.

❦

Henry sat uneasy at the bar.

"Didn't think we'd see you again," Matthew said as he came over to him.

Henry was shocked the man remembered him. "I had some business here in town to take care of," Henry said.

Matthew stuck out his hand. "Name's Matthew."

Henry shook his hand. "Henry."

"What'll it be?" Matthew asked.

"Whiskey."

Matthew smiled and turned for the whiskey bottle. He placed a glass in front of Henry and poured. "You got a place around here?"

"My brother does. I'm helping fix it up while he's gone."

"Oh, who's your brother?" Matthew asked.

"Sam Bower." Henry watched Matthew for a response.

"How's Beth and the boy doing?"

"They're all right, but there's some stuff that needs repair. I'm doing that for them while Sam's away."

"Any idea when he'll be—"

"Well, if it isn't the handsome stranger," Lauren said as she walked over to the bar, interrupting Matthew. Her green dress pushed her bosoms up slightly above the neckline, giving the appearance she would pop out if she bent over.

"Lauren, don't you have something to do or maybe someone to go see?" Matthew asked, tilting his head slightly toward the kitchen.

Lauren ignored Matthew and sat down next to Henry. "So, what brings you back to our place?" she asked.

"Just had some business to tend to." Henry swallowed what was left of his whiskey and put some money on the bar. "Thanks for the drink," he said to Matthew.

As Henry was about to walk out, Lucy came from somewhere in the back to get everyone for supper. She froze when she saw him. Lauren put her arm around Henry's and smiled toward Lucy, but Lucy saw his muscles tense at Lauren's touch.

Lucy took a deep breath and walked over to the bar. "Supper's ready if you want it hot," she said, looking at Matthew.

Lauren batted her eyes at Henry. "Why don't you join us again? I'll make it worth your while."

"No, thanks. I have to get back," Henry said, pulling his arm away from Lauren's and leaving as quickly as he could.

"Boy, Lucy, you sure know how to spoil things. I could have had him in my room for dessert if you hadn't come out here," Lauren teased.

"I don't see what I've got to do with it. Maybe you're not the sweet treat you think you are," Lucy said, leaving Lauren standing with her mouth wide open as she went back to the kitchen.

"Go tell the other girls supper is ready, Lauren," Matthew said, smiling. He was proud of Lucy for sticking up for herself.

He wondered about that Henry fellow. He didn't know Sam had a brother. In fact, the only thing Matthew knew about Sam was his love of money and women. And he felt certain that if Henry had ended up in Lauren's bed that would be the only thing those two had in common.

❖

Chapter Eight

Lucy hardly ate. She was distracted, curious as to why Henry had been in the saloon earlier.

"Lucy," Ms. Betty said, "are you feeling okay?"

"Hmm?" Lucy looked down at her plate, still full of food. "Oh, yes, ma'am. I'm fine. Just not very hungry."

"Well, you need to try to eat some of your dinner. I hate to see good food go to waste," Ms. Betty said.

"I bet she can't eat because she's thinking about the handsome stranger from the other day," Lauren said.

Lucy narrowed her eyes at Lauren.

"What handsome stranger?" Catherine asked.

"You remember, the one that had lunch with us," Lauren explained.

"Ooh, he was a good-looking man," Catherine said.

"Yeah, he was, and he was back today," Lauren continued.

"What's that?" Ms. Betty asked. She didn't like it when she didn't know anything about the men coming to see her girls.

Matthew cleared his throat and answered before Lauren could. "He came back in for a drink today. His name is Henry Bower."

Ms. Betty looked at Matthew. "Bower?"

"Sam Bower's brother," Matthew explained.

Ms. Betty's face reddened. "You tell him he's not welcome here the next time he tries to come in."

"Now, Betty," Matthew said, "we can't be rude to him. Henry hasn't done anything against us."

"He's a Bower. That should be a good enough reason."

"He may be a Bower, but I don't think he's anything like Sam," Matthew said. "Besides, I don't think we'll see too much of him." He looked at Lauren. "I don't take him for the type of man that would enjoy our establishment much."

"Oh, I could have gotten him up to my room if Lucy hadn't interrupted," Lauren said, smiling at Lucy.

"You know Ms. Betty doesn't like us being late to the table," Lucy said, trying to hold in her anger. "Besides, he didn't seem that interested in you."

"We both know he'd be more interested in me, Lucy," Lauren said. "You're too homely."

Tears welled up in Lucy's eyes. She knew she didn't have the beauty the other girls had, but she wasn't ugly.

"That's enough, Lauren," Matthew said sharply.

"May I be excused?" Lucy asked Ms. Betty.

"Of course, dear. I'll save your plate for a while in case you get hungry."

Lucy left the table and the saloon and turned toward the mercantile. She needed fresh air. Lauren's words had hurt her.

Matthew's words had hurt Lucy, too, though she knew he didn't do it intentionally. If Henry was too good for the saloon, then he was too good for her. She ran down an alley and fell to her knees crying.

"Am I really that ugly, both physically and inwardly?" Lucy wondered. "Am I not good enough for anyone? Where did I lose myself? What happened to the girl I once was? Aunt Judy had always stressed the importance of how a lady looked. I never thought I was ugly. I had men interested in me before I left, but then, I was all dressed up. I wasn't me. Is that what I have to do? Surely not. Papa had always said the important beauty came from within. Have I lost that beauty being here? Maybe by working my plan, I can find myself again."

&

Lucy didn't know how long she had been there crying when she felt a shadow start to fall over top of her. Her body tensed up in fear.

"Lucy," a voice said.

Lucy recognized the voice but refused to look in the direction of it. Instead, she wiped her face on her dress sleeve.

"Lucy," the voice said again, "are you okay?"

Henry squatted down to look at her, then reached out and turned her face toward his. Her eyes were red from fresh tears and her cheeks were splotchy.

"Lucy, please tell me what's wrong," he pleaded.

Lucy took a deep breath and tried to regain her composure. She moved her chin out of his grasp and said, "It's none of your concern." She stood up and attempted to smooth out her dress. "I have to get back," she said and walked away quickly.

It bothered her that Henry had caught her crying, yet when he had turned her face to him, there was a soft look in his deep brown eyes. Lucy shook her head. "He's too good for me. The good ones always are," she thought.

Henry stared after Lucy. It bothered him to see her like that, and he wanted to know who had caused her so much hurt.

Henry stood up. It was getting late, and he needed to get back to his brother's place. He hoped Lucy would be all right.

❦

Chapter Nine

Lucy woke the next morning ashamed of herself. She hated that Henry had seen her crying in the alley. It seemed every time she saw him, it was on awkward, unpleasant terms. She couldn't understand why Henry's opinion of her mattered.

"He probably thinks the same way about me that everyone else does," she thought, pulling herself out of bed and pouring fresh water into her basin to splash on her face.

A few hours later, Lucy walked with Wyatt down to the mercantile. It was Thursday, the day Ms. Betty usually picked up supplies, but she had sent Lucy in her place.

Lucy could see Mrs. DeWitt behind the counter taking a customer's order, so they stood in line to wait their turn. Mrs. DeWitt tried to focus on the customer before her, but her eyes kept drifting to the boy. By the time Lucy and Wyatt approached the counter with their order, Mrs. DeWitt couldn't deny how much he looked like her husband, William.

"Good morning, Mrs. DeWitt," Lucy said.

"Good morning," she responded, looking at Wyatt.

Wyatt tugged on Lucy's skirt. "Yes, Wyatt."

"Can I have some candy? Please, Lucy?"

"I'll buy you a couple of pieces, but you have to save them for this afternoon."

"Okay."

Lucy handed the list to Mrs. DeWitt, who looked at it and decided to call her husband from the back to help.

Mrs. DeWitt waited patiently until Mr. DeWitt came out from the back.

"I was working on paperwork," he said. "What could you possibly need my help with?"

Mrs. DeWitt pointed at Lucy and Wyatt. "They're here for Ms. Betty's weekly things. I'm not familiar with some of the items and thought you could help me since you fill the order most of the time."

Mr. DeWitt looked at Lucy. His eyes widened when he realized the little boy was there. He cleared his throat. "Sure, why don't I just fill the order, then and you can work on writing up the bill of sale."

Mrs. DeWitt had seen the shock wash across her husband's face when he noticed the boy. As he spoke, she looked closely at both man and boy. She could not deny that they were indeed father and son. For a moment, she was saddened that her husband had sought intimacy elsewhere, but as the moment passed, her heart filled with anger and she decided whatever Lucy had up her sleeve was worth investing in.

"Lucy," Mrs. DeWitt said, "why don't you come by the house tomorrow morning, and we'll discuss the possibility of a job here. I think I need to focus my efforts elsewhere for a while, and I obviously don't know everything I need to about the store anymore."

She knew her husband could hear her and would be curious as to why she was offering Lucy a job since she always enjoyed being in the store. She simply wasn't sure she could handle being there with him anymore, let alone being at home with him. She would be sure to work out a deal with Lucy to be told everything that lying cheat did from now on.

"How does that sound?" Mrs. DeWitt asked Lucy. "Would you like to work in the store for a while and get away from the stale air of the saloon?"

"Gee, Mrs. DeWitt, that sounds real nice," Lucy said. "I'll talk to Ms. Betty today, and I'll come by tomorrow morning to discuss things further."

"That sounds great," Mrs. DeWitt said as Mr. DeWitt put the final things on the counter and loaded up the basket Lucy and Wyatt had brought.

"Here is the bill of sale for Ms. Betty's records. Have a good day," Mr. DeWitt said as he pushed them toward the door.

"Wyatt, tell Mr. and Mrs. DeWitt bye and thank you for the candy," Lucy said.

"Bye. Thank you," Wyatt said around a mouthful of candy.

As they walked back to the saloon, Lucy smiled at what had just happened. Mrs. DeWitt could not deny Wyatt was her husband's bastard child, and it seemed that she was more than willing to help Lucy now.

❧

Chapter Ten

Henry tried to focus on fixing the fence, but the image of Lucy on her knees crying kept invading his thoughts. "She's just a saloon girl," he thought. "Why do I care?"

Something had seemed different about her when he had lunch with all of them that day. She wasn't like the other saloon girls. She was very pretty and there was something that made her stand out, but Henry just couldn't put his finger on it. He shook his head to clear his mind and focus on the work before him.

"Lucy, I just don't understand. Why do you feel the need to work at the mercantile?" Ms. Betty asked.

"I think I need a change of scenery. I'm not like the other girls here, and I'm actually quite thankful for that. I think my time will be better spent over there," Lucy tried to explain. She watched Ms. Betty as she sat silently for a moment, hoping her argument was strong enough to further her plan.

"Well," Ms. Betty finally said, "I won't argue that with you, but I've come to enjoy your help and your company. Could you work until the early afternoon and be back here to help me with supper?"

Lucy smiled. "Yes, ma'am. I don't see why that wouldn't work. I'll discuss it with Mrs. DeWitt in the morning." Lucy stood, went to the chair Ms. Betty was sitting in, bent down, and hugged her. "Thank you for understanding," Lucy said.

❧

Lucy woke Friday morning anxious to see what the day would bring. She couldn't wait to get to Mrs. DeWitt's place. Lucy ate breakfast quickly and went on her way.

She knocked on the door and once inside, she made herself comfortable in the chair Beatrice directed her to.

Mrs. DeWitt came in a few minutes later. "Good morning, Lucy," she said stiffly.

"Good morning," Lucy said and smiled.

Mrs. DeWitt sat in a chair across from Lucy. "Would you like some tea?" she asked.

"No, thank you." Lucy watched as Mrs. DeWitt took a deep breath. She was glad Mrs. DeWitt seemed uncomfortable. It was time for some of the high-falutin townspeople to be knocked off their pedestals.

"Mrs. DeWitt, I don't really have all morning, so if we could discuss what we need to so I can be on my way, that would be great."

Mrs. DeWitt's cheeks reddened, and she cleared her throat. "Okay, when would you like to start working at the store?"

"As soon as I can. That would be best, I think. Ms. Betty is okay with it as long as I'm off early enough to still help her with supper."

"Humph. I thought you wanted to be done with that place."

"Yes, that's my intention. But Ms. Betty is a good person, and I want to help her as much as I can. Besides, I'll still have to board there until I save enough to move somewhere else."

"All right," Mrs. DeWitt said. "Why don't you start Monday morning then?"

"I think that will work just fine," Lucy said, getting up to leave.

"One more thing before you go, Lucy," Mrs. DeWitt said.

Lucy sat back down. "Yes, ma'am."

"I'm doing you a favor by letting you work in the store."

Lucy nodded her head in agreement.

"Well, I would like you to do a favor for me," Mrs. DeWitt said.

"What's that?"

"I would like you to watch my husband. I want to know every little thing that man does from now on. Can you do that?"

"I can do that."

"Good. Then I'll see you Monday morning."

❧

Mrs. DeWitt went to her bedroom after Lucy left. Her husband's actions still made her shake with heartache. She couldn't understand what drew him to that saloon with those girls. Sure, she wasn't young anymore. Wrinkles had started to form on her brow a good year ago, and her hair had a little grey sprinkled through it. But she'd never had children, so she still had her figure. Besides, her husband was no spring chicken. Mr. DeWitt had his own wrinkles due to age and the stress of owning a business, and his midsection had blossomed where his wife's lacked. "Why, then, does he feel the need to seek...what does he seek there?" Mrs. De Witt wondered.

She lay down on her bed. The thought of it all brought on a headache, just as it had the day before. She wiped her eyes and shook her head. She wasn't the kind of woman that let things bother

her. Her house had never been one of scandal, but she suddenly felt swallowed by it. She couldn't even look at her husband anymore without becoming sick to her stomach.

Chapter Eleven

"Ouch!"

Henry looked up from the pile of wood he was cutting. Sammy was over by the barn holding one of his fingers.

"What happened?" Henry asked.

"That stinking tomcat bit me," Sammy answered.

"Let me look at it." Sammy held out his bleeding hand to Henry. "Go in and let your mama wash and doctor it."

As Sammy ran off toward the house, Henry looked around the yard at all the things that still needed mending. He was trying to pay and trade for things to keep his sister-in-law from going further into debt with the mercantile.

Henry wondered how his Charlotte was doing. He hadn't heard back from the telegram he'd sent her yet, and his brother hadn't responded to any of the ones Henry had sent him either.

Henry couldn't understand Sam's behavior or why it bothered him. Sam had always been that way—chasing what he couldn't, and shouldn't, have. Henry shook his head in frustration. He knew there was more going on than Beth had told him, and the bartender in the saloon seemed to know something. Henry remembered the look he gave him when Henry told him his full name. Maybe it was time to make another run into town for supplies and see exactly what the bartender knew.

❦

It was another Sunday morning at church, and Lucy found it hard to sit there, looking at all the hypocrites' backs.

She'd made eye contact with Mrs. DeWitt once and smiled and turned away, just as Mrs. DeWitt had done. It was a cordial exchange, neither woman really caring for the other.

The pianist began playing the first hymn and everyone stood. Pastor Tom went to the podium and led the church in song before beginning the service.

"Good morning, everyone," Pastor Tom said, eyeing the room before him carefully. All eyes in the congregation were looking up at him. He breathed in their anticipation and calmed himself with reassuring thoughts. "Everyone in town seeks me when there is a problem. They all trust my counsel. No one sitting before me thinks ill of me.

No one in attendance today knows my dirty little secret," he thought and smiled. It was time to deliver the weekly sermon—words carefully chosen to take his parishioners into the week and bring them back next Sunday.

♦

Lucy believed in God and knew most of what Pastor Tom said came from the Bible, but when he started talking about sin, she took issue with him. He would lean over the pulpit as if he were God Himself, condemning each person for breathing. Lucy had to keep from jumping up and yelling at him to look at himself before condemning others.

As soon as church was over, she left the stuffy building. She was suffocating in that pit of lies and needed the refreshment the cool breeze and sunshine offered.

When Mrs. DeWitt came out, Lucy took a deep breath and walked over to her. "I'll see you tomorrow morning, Mrs. DeWitt," she said and walked on, not intending to stick around for conversation. Mrs. DeWitt being uncomfortable in front of her friends was part of Lucy's plan.

"Oh, that girl!" Mrs. DeWitt thought, watching Lucy walk away and turning back to her friends, whose mouths were gaped open.

"What did she mean by that, Martha?" one of them asked.

All eyebrows were raised as they waited for Mrs. DeWitt's answer.

"She's going to start working at the mercantile," Mrs. DeWitt said.

Gasps echoed among the group. "What?" another asked, shocked.

"What on earth are you doing letting a harlot work for you?" Belinda asked.

Mrs. DeWitt was beside herself. She didn't want to answer questions, especially now that she needed that girl to keep an eye on her husband.

"Well, we decided....just recently...to have another person in the store so I'm more free to do other things. Lucy seemed like she would be good to have in there."

"Lucy?" Belinda asked. "When did you get on a first name basis with the town's harlots, Martha?"

"How dare you! I'm not on a first name basis with any of the rest of them, but I can't very well go around calling her 'Girl' all the time."

Mr. DeWitt called to his wife, telling her it was time to go.

"Good day," she said to the ladies and stomped away, feeling all her friends' eyes follow her.

♦

Chapter Twelve

Henry had forgotten it was Sunday until he saw people walking home from the town church. He chided himself for missing church...again but then he reminded himself that God had nothing to offer him since He'd taken his wife away.

He figured the mercantile wouldn't be open on a Sunday, so he decided to go to the saloon.

When Matthew looked his way, Henry spoke. "Wasn't sure you'd be open, it being Sunday," Henry said.

"Our customers don't care what day of the week it is as long as they can drink and gamble."

"Among other things," Henry said to himself as he caught sight of Lucy going toward the back of the saloon.

"What'll you have?" Matthew asked.

"Whiskey."

Matthew could sense that Henry wanted to talk, but his years of bartending had taught him to always let the customer have the lead. So he waited.

Henry took a deep breath. It was now or never. "So, how well do you know my brother?" he asked.

Matthew was cleaning a glass with a towel. He stopped for a minute and thought. "I'd say I know him pretty good," Matthew said. "Why do you ask?"

"Just curious." Henry sipped on his whiskey, unable to determine if it was the whiskey or the taste of the words he was holding back burning his throat.

Matthew put down the glass and slung the towel over his left shoulder. Henry looked at him, unsure if he wanted to finish the conversation he had started, but Matthew was waiting for whatever he had to say next.

"Was he a regular around here?" Henry finally asked.

"You might say that." Matthew picked up another glass to clean.

"What was his...main...activity...here?"

Matthew continued to clean the glass, turning it slowly in his hands. "Are you sure you want these answers, son?" he asked. "I don't see how they would help you or his family any."

Henry tossed back the rest of the whiskey in his glass. "Yeah, I need to know if my brother was still the rotten piece of flesh he'd always been." Henry watched Matthew's eyes get big in response to the comment he made. "So was he?" Henry asked.

Matthew stopped cleaning the second glass and sighed, looking at Henry. "Your brother cheated people every time he was in here. If he wasn't cheating at cards, he was convincing some poor fool about rumors of a silver mine somewhere nearby. He got drunk every time he came in." Matthew took a breath. "And yes, he went upstairs a few times. I put a stop to that, though, once he took to slapping one of the girls."

"When he left," Henry said, "did he leave alone?"

Matthew looked down and shook his head, then looked at Henry dead-on. "No. He left with one of the girls."

"That bastard," Henry said, slamming his fist on the bar.

"As far as I know, Beth doesn't know that part," Matthew continued.

Henry's face began to burn with anger. "If she knows my brother, she won't be surprised by it. Did he imply that he would be coming back?"

"I don't know what his intentions were, but the girl he left with said she would never come back here."

Henry twirled the glass between his hands on the bar. "Tell me, Matthew, did he owe a lot of money to anybody?"

"Yeah," Matthew said as he continued cleaning glasses.

"Who?" Henry asked.

"Me," Matthew said.

"You?" Henry asked. "Why does Sam owe you money?"

"For starters, he wrecked my bar during one of his drunken fits," Matthew replied.

Henry sucked in a deep breath and lifted his glass toward Matthew. "Can I have another?" While Matthew poured more whiskey, Henry continued. "You said, 'for starters.' What else does he owe you money for?"

"The bill for the girl he hit," Matthew said.

Henry's brown eyes went wide. "What happened with the girl, Matthew? What aren't you telling me?"

Matthew put down the last glass he was cleaning. "Right before your lousy brother hightailed it out of here, he came in to gamble and be with his usual girl." Matthew wrung the rag around his hands. "Well, his usual girl was with someone else at the time. The only girl that was available didn't really have a lot of experience with men, and your brother was a hard and vicious man." Matthew looked down at his now white hands and let go of the rag. "They were in her room, and I guess she didn't do quite as he wanted. I ran up there when I heard a loud crashing sound and found her passed out on the floor by her dresser. Her head was bleeding."

Henry could feel his pulse quickening.

"Sam was over her with his hand back, about to strike her again. I grabbed him from behind and punched him until he was out. When he came to, he found himself sitting with his hands tied up on the back of a wagon. I told him that if he ever came in here again, I'd kill him. He hasn't stepped foot in here since," Matthew finished.

Henry was angry. "And the girl? How was she?"

"Lucy is fine now, but we don't really let the men go to her room anymore. She's Ms. Betty's helper now."

"Lucy! It was Lucy my brother hurt," Henry thought, feeling like he was going to be sick. He needed to get out of there. He got up off the barstool and laid some money for his drinks down on the counter. "Thanks for being honest with me, Matthew," he said.

"Look, Henry, you need to know that no one in this town is missing him, and I'm probably not the only one here that's willing to kill him on sight. I don't know what you intend to do about him and his family, but you should know he's not welcome here, and I'd be careful about saying you're related to him if I were you."

"Thanks. I'm not quite sure what I'm going to do about any of this mess yet," Henry said as he walked out of the saloon and bent over by his horse. He sucked in a big gulp of air. His brother was a real piece of work.

He saw Lucy round the corner as he got in his wagon to leave. He wished he hadn't told her about being related to Sam. He wanted to talk to her and tell her he was sorry for what his brother had done to her, but he turned his horse and wagon and headed back to his brother's dilapidated ranch.

❧

Chapter Thirteen

Lucy had seen Henry at the bar when she went into the kitchen and wondered why he was there. She wanted to peek out at him but wasn't able to from where she was. Ms. Betty had her peeling potatoes by the back door. If Lucy leaned forward just enough, she could see part of Henry's shirt on his left shoulder. When she nearly fell over from watching, she chided herself. "What do I care if he is here in the saloon? He's a man, and I know why men come here." She sighed and went back to peeling potatoes, wishing Henry was different.

Lucy watched Henry ride out of town and wondered what he had talked about with Matthew. Whatever it was, Henry hadn't looked happy about it.

She had seen him look her way when she came around the corner. Something inside Lucy wanted Henry to call out to her, but Lauren's ugly words from the other day came at her: "Lucy is plain. There isn't anything special about her. Her hair is dark like an Indian and her skin ghostly pale."

She reached up to tuck a strand of hair behind her ear, her hand lingering over the scar Sam left.

Lucy shuddered as she remembered that day. Sam had been very drunk and very angry that Heather wasn't available. Lucy didn't like the idea of being with any man in the way a saloon girl was expected to be, and Sam was just horrid.

When he entered her room, he began getting rough with her. Lucy remembered him muttering something, but the only thing she heard clearly was how he was taking Heather and leaving this godforsaken place for the "promise land," as he called it. Then he slapped her so hard she fell and hit her forehead against the corner of the bureau, knocking trinkets off the top of it.

She passed out somewhere between hitting the bureau and the floor. When she came to, she found herself in bed with Ms. Betty fussing over her and Matthew pacing the room. Mike, the town barber and makeshift doctor, was there, too, putting a large bandage over the cut on her forehead.

Lucy had never seen Matthew so angry. Mike had pulled him and Ms. Betty aside to tell them about Lucy's injury. Lucy had watched them, and she remembered Matthew's face turning a deep red.

†

As Lucy walked back into the saloon, she thought about how Henry had looked. From her spot at the back door, she could barely see him, but even at that distance, she could tell his jaw was set, his eyes were focused on Matthew, and his face had burned red as he got up to leave.

Lucy wasn't sure what had sent her outside when she saw Henry get off the barstool. She just remembered giving some kind of excuse to Ms. Betty and leaving. She hadn't really been aware of what she was doing until she saw Henry in his wagon.

She could see the muscles working under his shirt as he maneuvered the horses and wagon, and a shudder had run through her as she took in every part of him.

Experiencing feelings like this for a man was new to her, and she wasn't sure what to do with them. But then she remembered the disdain Henry had toward the saloon and those who worked there and reminded herself that he had no interest in her. "Why should he?" she thought to herself. "I'm not anything special."

The saloon had blemished who she was. It didn't matter what she did to earn her keep there, she was associated with those people.

"Tomorrow, things start changing for me," she thought, heading into the kitchen to finish helping Ms. Betty with supper.

Lucy had been on Henry's mind the whole way back to the ranch. He knew she had seen him as he left. He could feel her eyes on his back. "Those sky-blue eyes," he thought. He had been tempted to look back at her but forced himself not to.

Henry had seen the scar the day he found her crying in the alley, but he hadn't paid much attention to it at the time. He had been too distracted by finding her that way. He hadn't understood then why it bothered him so much, but he did now. He liked Lucy. There was something about her he found intriguing, and every time he looked at her, he fell into her blue eyes.

Henry shook his head as he entered the ranch gates. He found it hard to believe that he and his brother were even related. Both were raised to earn a decent living the good, honest way. Sam had always had that bug for chasing after the impossible, though—moving on to the next big thing, not caring who he destroyed along the way.

Henry used to secretly wish Sam hadn't married and had a child. He had even tried to talk Beth out of it one day when he had seen her in town, but she wouldn't hear of it. She was too in love with the image Sam presented to her.

Henry knew it was only a matter of time before Sam would break Beth's heart, and now here he was, trying to clean up his older brother's mess...again. "Maybe I shouldn't this time," he thought. "Maybe I should just go back home to my daughter and forget about all of this."

He missed Charlotte terribly, but he knew he couldn't leave Beth and Sammy with how things were. He was a better man than his lousy brother. He would figure out what was best for them and do what he could.

An idea occurred to Henry as he put the horse and wagon away. Maybe he knew just what to do for them.

Chapter Fourteen

Lucy rose early Monday, dressed quickly, and went downstairs to the kitchen. She'd agreed to help Ms. Betty with breakfast and other preparations for the day, as usual, before going to the mercantile to work. Lucy felt Ms. Betty was afraid of losing her, so she hoped to keep her busy.

Together, they prepared pancakes and made sure there was plenty of coffee, and Lucy milked the cow they kept in the back just to make sure Wyatt got plenty of milk to drink.

She went upstairs to wake all the girls, and everyone responded except Lauren. Lucy knocked on her door again, and Wyatt came out with his hair a mess and his shirt partially untucked, trying to tug his suspenders up onto his shoulders.

"Mama is still asleep," he told Lucy.

She peeked in and could see Lauren in bed, but something didn't feel right. Lucy sent Wyatt downstairs to get his breakfast, and she tiptoed into the room. "Lauren," she whispered, but Lauren didn't move, so Lucy moved closer. "Lauren, it's time to get up."

Still nothing, so Lucy moved closer to the bed and noticed Lauren was soaking wet. Lucy touched her forehead with a tentative hand. Lauren was burning up, but she stirred from the touch, opened her eyes slightly, looked toward Lucy, rolled over with a groan, and went back to sleep.

Lucy ran down the stairs, bumping into Matthew, who was walking toward the kitchen.

"What the devil?" Matthew said. "What's the rush, Lucy?"

"Sorry, Matthew." Lucy stopped and turned toward him. "I was going to get Ms. Betty. Something is wrong with Lauren. She won't wake up and is soaked."

Matthew's face registered alarm. "Go tell Betty. I'll go get Mike," Matthew said, turning toward the door.

&

Lucy walked to the mercantile for her first day of work. She hoped the day would not be as crazy there as it had been at the saloon so far.

All the girls had heard her tell Ms. Betty about Lauren. Everyone was in a panic because getting sick could mean an early date with death, especially with no real doctor around. Mike was the closest thing they had, and while his efforts were appreciated, everyone secretly wished a doctor would arrive someday soon.

Lucy had heard Mike talking to Matthew and Ms. Betty as she was leaving. Mike admitted he wasn't sure exactly what Lauren had. Her symptoms were fever, sweating, and shivering. Her skin was pale and clammy, and she had a horrible-sounding cough. He suggested keeping a cool cloth on her head to break the fever and giving her broth or water as she would take it.

Wyatt would stay with Ms. Betty, who had a home separate from the saloon, until Lauren recovered.

&

"Good to see you believe in being on time," Mrs. DeWitt said to Lucy curtly when she arrived.

"Just trying to start off on the right foot," Lucy said.

Mrs. DeWitt motioned for Lucy to follow her to the counter. She pulled an apron out from underneath it. "Wear this while you work. You never know what you could possibly be doing, and this will protect your clothes some." Lucy put the apron on, and Mrs. DeWitt said, "I saw Mike and Matthew hurrying to the saloon this morning. Anything the matter?"

"Lauren's sick," Lucy answered.

Mrs. DeWitt's hand went to her chest. "And the boy? Is he sick too?"

"No, ma'am. Just Lauren. Wyatt will stay with Ms. Betty until Lauren's better."

Mrs. DeWitt realized she had been holding her breath and slowly let it out. "Well, that's good. I hate to see someone so young get sick out here." She took another breath and tried to regain her composure. "Now, let's get started. There's a lot to show you."

By lunchtime, Lucy had been shown all the different fabrics, tools, and other essentials that the mercantile sold. When customers occasionally came in, Mrs. DeWitt had Lucy watch her.

Lucy was allowed to go home for her lunch break. When she reached the saloon, she found a quarantine sign on the door. She stepped up, peeked over the swinging door, and saw Matthew working at the bar.

"Matthew!" she called out. "What's going on? Why is the saloon quarantined?"

Matthew looked up and walked over to the door. "Mike came back about an hour ago to check on Lauren, and she's gotten worse. He's concerned she may have something contagious and wants to keep people away from here until we know for sure."

Lucy put her hand on the door so she could go in, but Matthew stopped her.

"You can't come in, Lucy. Mike said everyone in the building had to stay in and anyone who wasn't here had to stay out."

"But, where am I supposed to stay?" she asked. "What about my clothes and things?"

"I'll have Cynthia pack a bag for you. Maybe you can stay with Ms. Betty. She wasn't here when Mike put the sign up and since she's keeping Wyatt, we felt it best they stay at her place until this is over. I'm sorry, Lucy. Lauren being sick puts all of us out one way or another, but I need to protect all of you as best I can. The girls and I are cleaning this place top to bottom. Mike said to do that just in case it's something in here that got her sick." Matthew put his hand on her shoulder. "Go see Ms. Betty. She's probably working on lunch. She's going to bring down some soup for all of us. I'm sure she'll let you stay with her, and I'll have your bag ready to give her when she comes."

❧

Ms. Betty didn't seem to mind at all when Lucy asked if she could stay with her.

After Lucy, Ms. Betty, and Wyatt all had a bowl of soup, Ms. Betty packed up some to take down to the saloon. Lucy took Wyatt with her to the store.

Mrs. DeWitt had a puzzled look on her face when Lucy walked in with Wyatt.

"He has to stay with me until Ms. Betty is done delivering soup to the saloon. Mike put a quarantine sign on the door, so the three of us are shut out until he takes it down," Lucy explained.

Mrs. DeWitt looked down at Wyatt. "Well, I guess it's all right this one time," she said, looking up at Lucy, "but we can't make a habit of it. We'll resume your training once he's gone. For now, go practice folding the fabric like I showed you this morning."

&

Chapter Fifteen

By the next morning, news had traveled through town that Lauren had died during the night. To most, her death didn't matter. She was just a saloon girl after all. There were some, though, that did mourn her loss over the next few weeks. Lucy had seen Mr. DeWitt's eyes mist several times when he thought she couldn't see him.

It was decided that Wyatt would live with Ms. Betty. He didn't quite understand why his mom wasn't around anymore. Matthew had told him he would see her again one day, many years after he had become a big, strong man and that seemed to work. Wyatt started doing things he thought would make him a "big, strong man" sooner.

Mike had kept the quarantine sign up for a while to make sure no one else fell ill, and all of Lauren's linens were burned for fear of contamination. Lucy moved back into the saloon two weeks after Lauren died.

The saloon was packed within thirty minutes after Mike took the quarantine sign off the door, despite town wives hoping their men wouldn't visit when it reopened.

Lucy was getting the hang of working at the mercantile, and truth be told, she liked it a lot more than working at the saloon. She felt Mrs. DeWitt was starting to warm up to her but noticed the rigid woman kept her distance when her friends were around.

Lucy felt her plan was going quite well, though slowly. She needed Mrs. DeWitt's and her friends' backing in order for it to work. The next step was a big one, and Lucy needed it to work.

She had been waiting for a chance to talk to Mrs. DeWitt. Finally, one slow afternoon, Lucy decided it was time. She finished sweeping the floor, put the broom away, and walked over to the counter where Mrs. DeWitt was finishing up with a customer.

"Mrs. DeWitt, I was wondering," Lucy began when the customer had left.

This part of the plan scared her. She needed Mrs. DeWitt to be okay with what she wanted to do.

Mrs. DeWitt looked at her. "Yes."

"I was wondering if anyone lives upstairs."

"No. No one does right now. Why?"

"Well, I've been thinking about moving out of the saloon." Lucy saw Mrs. DeWitt squint her eyes in thought, and she rushed on. "I mean, since I'm not really one of them anymore. I just thought I could make it official and move out of the saloon."

Mrs. DeWitt thought for a minute.

"I don't know, Lucy. I don't know if I like the idea of a girl living upstairs alone, and I couldn't condone male company," she added.

"No, ma'am. I wouldn't think of having male company in my place unsupervised." Lucy couldn't help not ruling it out completely. "You and Mr. DeWitt live right next door, so I wouldn't really be alone."

Mrs. DeWitt sighed and took a long look at Lucy. "I need to think about it, Lucy, and I also need to talk to Mr. DeWitt about it."

"Yes, ma'am. I understand that, but I do hope you'll let me live there. I'll even pay rent if need be."

Lucy picked up a dusting cloth and went about straightening shelves. She knew not to push any further and felt confident the DeWitts would let her live up there. Lucy was almost giddy with anticipation. She decided it was a great day and started humming until she heard a familiar voice behind her.

&

Henry walked into the mercantile with the list of supplies he needed for Beth's place. He wanted the store clerk to gather the items on the list while he went to find out if any telegrams came in for him, but he didn't see anyone at the counter. When he heard humming coming from the back corner, he walked over to sound.

"Excuse me," he said.

Henry's eyes widened when he saw Lucy turn around and look up at him.

"Can I help you?" she asked.

Henry lost his voice for a minute, then cleared his throat and spoke. "Lucy, what are you doing here?"

"I work here," she said and lifted her chin a little.

"Oh" was all Henry could manage to get out.

"So, can I help you with something?" she asked.

Her words snapped Henry out of his daze.

"I have a list of things I need," he said.

"Okay, I can fill the order for you."

"If it's all right, I have another errand I need to do while you're gathering it all up."

"That'll be fine. I'll have it all ready for you to load when you get back."

Henry turned to go but thought better of it and turned back to Lucy. He tipped his hat to her, said thank you, and walked out.

❧

Lucy laughed as she gathered the stuff for Henry. She had seen his cheeks redden when he realized he was talking to her. She could tell it put him off to see her working there. "Good!" she thought. She was tired of people assuming things about her just because she lived in the saloon. That was one reason Lucy wanted to move out.

She pictured Henry using each item she found for him. In her mind, she could see his muscles flexing as he worked. The thought made Lucy blush.

The last item on the list was material—a floral print. "Why does he need a floral print? Who is the girl in his life that needs this?" she wondered.

Lucy suddenly felt embarrassed and ashamed for the thoughts she'd had about Henry. "I should have known he has a girl," she scolded herself. "Why wouldn't he? He is a very handsome man." She knew looks didn't make the man, but they sure helped.

❧

Chapter Sixteen

Henry had two telegrams waiting for him at the telegraph office. One was from his parents. It was a happy message with a quick update about Charlotte. Oh, how he missed his little girl! The next one was from only his father.

It read:

Henry,

Forget your brother. Come home. Bring Beth and Sammy with you. Your brother is not worth the effort anymore.

Dad

He knew his father meant well, but it just wasn't that easy. For one, he wasn't sure his sister-in-law wanted to go back to Texas. And Henry also knew his brother needed to be dealt with, so he decided to send his brother another telegram, almost forgetting the other telegram in his hand.

It was from Sam, and it read:

Henry,

Stop bothering me. I'm not coming back and I'm not sending money. Beth can manage on her own. Go home and leave my family alone.

This news infuriated Henry. He walked up to the telegram window and asked to send a new telegram.

"Have it read, 'Sam, you are right. Beth can manage on her own. I will make sure the divorce is swift and painless for her. Henry.'"

Henry paid for the telegram and walked out. He was still fuming when he went back into the mercantile to pick up his items.

"Are my packages ready?" he asked Lucy as he walked up to the counter.

Lucy kept her face down. "Yes, here is your bill of sale."

Henry looked at the amount and dug money out of his pants pocket. "Here."

Henry tried to look at Lucy and smile, but she wouldn't make eye contact with him as she had only a little bit ago. "Why," Henry wondered, "is she friendly at first and then almost icy cold?" He shook his head. She wasn't worth the worry. He had more important things to take care of.

❦

Lucy watched as he loaded his wagon and left without saying another word to her. The flexing of his muscles made her cheeks flush. He had seemed upset when he came back to the mercantile. She wondered why but she couldn't look at him knowing he had a girl, and that hurt her.

"Lucy," Mrs. DeWitt called from the back room.

Lucy shook her head to clear her thoughts. "Coming, Mrs. DeWitt."

Lucy entered the small room behind the store. A small table and chairs sat in its center, and shelves lined three walls for extra store goods. The fourth wall was home to a wood-burning stove that was used in the winter.

Mrs. DeWitt was sitting at the table with Mr. DeWitt. "Have a seat, Lucy," she said.

Lucy sat down, unsure of what was about to happen.

"Mr. DeWitt and I have discussed it and we have decided that you can live upstairs."

"Oh, thank you," Lucy began, but Mrs. DeWitt held up her hand to stop her.

"There are some things we need to go over before you move in," Mrs. DeWitt continued.

"Yes, ma'am."

"First, it'll need a proper cleaning before you move in. We can start on that this afternoon after you're done working in the store. There isn't much furniture, but it has the few essentials—a bed, table, bureau. There is a small stove up there. Mr. DeWitt is going to make sure it works properly for you so you can cook your meals and such. We want it understood that there will absolutely be no male visitors up there for any reason."

"Yes, ma'am. I understand. There won't be," Lucy replied.

Lucy heard the store door chime and stood up to answer it. Before leaving the small room, she thanked the DeWitts again and went to wait on the customer.

❧

Lucy went to bed happy that night, knowing she would be leaving the saloon soon. The room wasn't too bad. It wouldn't take her and Mrs. DeWitt long to get it manageable enough to live in.

She told Matthew and Ms. Betty after supper that she would be moving above the store. While they both seemed saddened by the news, they were happy for her. Ms. Betty even admitted it was probably what was best for Lucy.

As she lay in bed thinking about how her life was about to change, Lucy's mind drifted to Henry.

She wished he didn't have a girl. Although she hardly knew him, something about him made her want to be his girl. Maybe it was the way his eyes softened when he looked at her, like he cared for her somehow.

Lucy shook her head. That was wishful thinking. Tears formed in Lucy's eyes as she realized just how much she had hoped to be his girl, but she told herself it was for the best.

♦

Henry was having a hard time sleeping that night too. Every time he closed his eyes, either Sam or Lucy came into view.

All Sam cared about was money, beer, and girls. How he ever fooled Beth about himself long enough to get her to marry him Henry would never know.

Then there was Lucy. He had thought she was beautiful since the first time he laid eyes on her. She wasn't all done up like the other girls at the saloon. Her hair was down, hugging her waist. He had never seen hair so black, and her eyes were so blue, he'd noticed when his met hers. Her fair complexion enhanced her eye and hair color even further. She wasn't very tall, he decided. Her head met him at his chest. "Perfect for hugging close," he thought.

He shook his head. He couldn't think of her that way, not when she always turned cold toward him and when he knew it was his brother that put the scar on her forehead. He needed to forget her. But, how could he do that? She worked at the mercantile now. He wouldn't be able to avoid her when he had to pick up supplies.

Henry rolled over. He wished his brother had never left Beth and that he had never come here and left Charlotte behind. But most of all, he wished he had never met Lucy because now she was all he really wanted.

Chapter Seventeen

It was nearing a month since Lucy had moved into the room above the mercantile. She was enjoying having a place to herself with no drunks lurking around, waiting to strike. She would never admit it to anyone, but she had been afraid another man would walk in her room at the saloon and slap her like Sam had but as she was sleeping.

As much as she tried to forget that day, the scar on her forehead etched it forever into her memory. She believed no man would ever want a scarred woman to keep as his wife. It is easy to forget someone's past without a visible reminder of it, but her scar would forever tell her past to anyone who saw it.

She started wearing her hair down more after that horrible day because it had a tendency to fall in her face and helped hide the wretched reminder. Admittedly, her hair got in the way when she waited on customers, but Lucy just tucked a little back behind her ear so the scar would still be hidden. That had worked until today.

Mrs. DeWitt had been watching Lucy with a customer from across the store. She felt Lucy's hair hanging in her face made her look unkempt and sloppy. Lucy was a pretty girl, and Mrs. DeWitt didn't understand why she wore her hair like that.

"Lucy, why don't you pin your hair up? I'm sure it would be much easier to work that way," Mrs. DeWitt suggested when they were having lunch in the small room behind the store.

"It doesn't bother me. I like it down. It's too heavy all heaped up on top of my head."

Mrs. DeWitt got up from her chair and went to stand behind Lucy. She reached out and gently pulled strands of Lucy's hair back away from her face. When she had only about half of it pulled back, she asked, "What if you wore it like this?"

Mrs. DeWitt, still standing over Lucy, was waiting for an answer when she saw the scar peeking out from her hair. She let go of what she had done and sat back down. Lucy had remained silent the entire time.

Trying to be gentle, Mrs. DeWitt asked, "Is the scar why you won't wear it up?"

Lucy nodded as tears formed in her eyes, and Mrs. DeWitt's tone softened a bit more. She was starting to care about Lucy, although she wouldn't admit that to anyone.

"Lucy, tell me how you got the scar," she prodded.

"No, Mrs. DeWitt. I'd rather not."

"I'm not going to judge you, Lucy."

Tears were flowing freely from Lucy's eyes. Mr. DeWitt had been quiet the entire time, watching his wife and Lucy.

"Martha, if she doesn't want to talk about it, she doesn't have to."

Lucy turned and looked at him, then looked back at Mrs. DeWitt. Something akin to anger flashed in her eyes as she looked from him to her.

"It was Sam Bower. His usual girl wasn't free. He was drunk and demanded to go to my room. He told me to do something. I didn't quite understand what he said, and before I could get him to repeat himself, he backhanded me so hard I hit my dresser and was knocked unconscious," Lucy spat.

Mrs. DeWitt gasped.

"When I came to, Matthew, Betty, and Mike were all there. Sheriff Daniel was there, too. I'd never seen Matthew so mad. Sam left town not long after that."

Mrs. DeWitt reached out and put her hand on Lucy's tear-stained cheek. "You poor dear," she said. "Men can be so cruel." She glanced at her husband. "You shouldn't be ashamed of it, though,

Lucy. You're a very pretty girl. That scar is minuscule compared to the beauty that radiates from you."

"I don't see that. I am ashamed of it. I feel like everyone sees it and forever marks me as a saloon girl."

"Oh no, dear. You are what you believe yourself to be. If you believe you are a saloon girl, then you will always be a saloon girl. It's your perception that matters."

Mrs. DeWitt got up again and went to a shelf that held extra ribbon. She found some scissors nearby and cut a piece off the spool. She came back over to Lucy and pulled her hair away from her face once again. She tied the ribbon around what she had gathered, leaving it a little loose so some would fall over the scar. When she was done, she found a small mirror and showed Lucy.

"There. See, you can still hide your scar and pull your hair back. Now it won't be in the way while you're working. Go upstairs and clean your face so you can get back to work."

Once upstairs in her room, Lucy sat down on the side of her bed for a moment. She couldn't believe she had actually told the DeWitts what had happened to her. She had never planned to share that with anyone, not even Melissa.

She took a few breaths to calm herself, went over to her wash basin, poured fresh water into it, and splashed her face, careful not to get her dress wet. As she dried her face, she looked in the mirror at herself.

Mrs. DeWitt had done a good job keeping the scar covered. Only the front part of her hair was pulled back, leaving the rest to hang down. Lucy ran her brush through the hair that was free from the ribbon. She was amazed at how good it really did look. She breathed a silent word of thanks for Mrs. DeWitt's kindness and went back downstairs to work.

❧

Chapter Eighteen

Henry had needed to go into town for supplies for a good week now. He just couldn't get up the nerve to see Lucy again because every encounter he'd had with her so far had ended sourly. When he lay down to sleep each night, he replayed every time he had been around her, but he couldn't come up with anything that would explain why she always turned on him. Her smile brightened his mood. He just wished he knew why it vanished when he was around.

Sitting down to write out his list for tomorrow's trip into town, Henry shook her from his head.

"What's bothering you?" Beth asked from the stove where she stirred their supper.

Henry looked up. "Nothing."

Beth looked at him. He knew she didn't believe him. "Want to try again?" she asked.

"I'm just trying to think of what all I need to get in town tomorrow."

Beth looked over at the curtains she had sewn with the fabric he had brought home the last time.

They sure did spruce the place up some. "Could you get some more fabric?" she asked. "I need to make some more pants for Sammy. He'll be outgrowing his soon."

"Sure, just write what you need on the list," Henry said, sliding the paper across the table to her.

Beth walked over to add fabric and a couple of other things to it. "Are you sure you're okay, Henry?" she asked.

"Yeah, I'm fine, Beth," he said, not looking at her.

"I know what a burden Sammy and I have been. I wouldn't blame you if you wanted go back home. Charlotte probably misses you quite a bit."

"You are not a burden. I still don't understand why you won't pack up and go back with me though."

Henry and Beth had discussed all of them going back to Texas together, but Beth had said no from the start.

"This is our home, Henry," she pleaded. "This is the place that was built for Sammy and me. Somehow or another, I'm going to make it work for us."

"You can make a home for yourselves back in Texas. Charlotte would love for her cousin to be nearby."

"Henry, I know you mean well, but please don't ask again."

Beth turned back to the pot on the stove, and Henry shook his head again. He didn't seem to understand much of anything lately as far as women were concerned.

He finished writing out his list and went to freshen up just as Beth called Sammy in for supper. Sammy came up behind him, waiting his turn. Beth had bowls of stew waiting for them when they returned.

Henry said grace and a silent prayer of his own that Lucy would open up to him and that Beth would decide to go to Texas. Henry felt that was what was best for her and Sammy, but he knew she had to make that decision herself.

Lucy was sweeping the store floor and had just made it to the door when boots appeared on the boardwalk. She looked up and caught her breath. Henry was standing before her.

"Good morning, Lucy," Henry said.

Lucy looked into his brown eyes as they took her in. "Good morning, Henry," she almost whispered.

"I have a list of supplies I need to fill," he said to her.

Lucy took a breath and took the list from him. "Okay, I'll get started on it."

She turned and walked to the room behind the store to put the broom away. When she came out, Henry had moved closer to the counter.

"I need to run an errand."

"Okay, I'll get all this together for you while you're gone."

Henry stepped out onto the boardwalk. He needed to see if any telegrams had come for him. "Lucy sure is pretty today," he thought, starting across the street. "That's a real pretty way she's wearing her hair. Hides the scar just right."

Henry jumped out of his thoughts at the sound of horses galloping down the street. He looked up to see the stagecoach. He let it pass and crossed the street to the telegram office.

There had not been any response to the last telegram he'd sent Sam. As he made his way back to the mercantile, he glanced toward where the stagecoach had stopped. Though he was at a distance, Henry could tell the silhouette of the man before him belonged to his brother.

"What the hell is he doing here?" Henry mumbled to himself.

As much as he didn't want to see him, Henry had to find out why Sam was back. He watched as Sam helped a woman out of the stagecoach. Henry noticed how he kept a protective arm around her waist and wondered if she was the woman he had run off with. He saw Sam look in his direction and then motion to the woman for the two of them to go into the saloon.

"Great," Henry thought. "Just great."

Henry wasn't sure what he wanted to do or say. Sam hadn't bothered to send a telegram, and Henry wondered if he'd even received the last one he had sent him.

❧

"Get out!"

Henry could hear Matthew yelling from the street. He went to the door quickly and walked inside. Matthew was standing just inside the saloon, nose to nose with Sam.

"Get out of my place. You're not welcome here," Matthew said.

Sam stood there with a sly smile on his face.

"He always agitates people," Henry thought.

"Now, Matthew, I know we've had our differences, but surely you don't mean to be this way with an old friend," Sam said.

Henry, seeing Matthew's hand ball into a fist at his side, reached out and grabbed his brother by the arm and said, "Let's go, Sam."

Sam looked at him as if for the first time. "Oh, hey there, baby brother. Let's have a drink."

Henry pulled Sam to the door. "No, you have a wife and son waiting for you. Remember them?" Henry looked at the woman gathering her things to go with them. "You should stay in the hotel here until the stage leaves again. You won't want to miss it since you're not staying around," Henry said to her. He nodded to Matthew, who took the woman's things and started out the door with them. The woman hesitantly followed, looking to Sam for direction.

"Henry, that wasn't very nice. She's my traveling companion."

"I'm glad you had someone to keep you company while you traveled, Sam, but now it's time to go see Beth and Sammy."

Sam made a sour face as if being sobered by the mention of his family. "Fine. I got a bone to pick with that woman anyway."

Henry tightened his grip on his brother's arm and pulled him closer. "You listen here. I don't know why you're back and I don't know what you're planning, but if you touch them at all, I'll break every bone in your body."

Sam looked at his brother. "All right already. Let's go," he said.

Henry let go of Sam. "I have to get supplies from the mercantile first."

As he said it, Henry remembered Lucy worked there and he didn't want Sam going in there with him, so when they got to the wagon, Henry told him to wait there.

"I gave them my list already. I should just have to load up the wagon. Shouldn't be but just a minute," Henry said as he walked into the mercantile.

"Sorry, I took longer than expected," Henry said to Lucy.

"That's all right. It gave me time to get everything together and wait on her." Lucy motioned toward the woman and child headed to out of the store. "I haven't seen Ms. Betty and Wyatt in a while."

"I'm glad it worked out then."

Lucy handed him the bill of sale and Henry paid for it. As he gathered up the first load to take to the wagon, he heard his brother's voice.

"Henry, I thought you were only going to be a minute."

Henry watched as Lucy's eyes went wide. Though there was a counter between them, Henry moved in front of her in hopes of shielding her from Sam.

"I'm coming. Go back to the wagon," Henry said, but Sam continued forward.

"You obviously have more than one load to carry. Let me help." Sam reached for a pile, picked it up, and looked at Lucy. "Well now, aren't you a pretty little thing? I can see why my brother was taking so long."

Henry watched Lucy put her hand on her scar. She was shaking. "Leave her alone, Sam. Let's go."

"What? I'm not doing anything but paying a compliment to a pretty lady."

Henry looked at Lucy again and then back at his brother. His cheeks were starting to burn. "You've done plenty, Sam. Now let's go. Beth and Sammy will be glad to see you."

Henry's tone was sharp. He wanted to get Sam out of there away from Lucy as fast as possible. Sam seemed to sense his brother's anger and left with the rest of the Henry's things.

Henry turned back to Lucy. "I'm sorry he bothered you," he said gently.

Henry put his load down on the counter and reached across. He placed his hand where Lucy's had been, gently touching her scar. He then moved his hand under her chin and lifted her face to meet his eyes.

"He'll never bother you again, not as long as I can help it," Henry said, caressing her chin and gently brushing away a tear that had escaped her eyes.

He was about to lean across the counter and kiss her when Mrs. DeWitt came out from the back. Henry dropped his hand to hers and squeezed it real quick.

"Bye, Lucy."

"B-bye," Lucy stuttered, staring at the door Henry had just walked through, trying to figure out what had just happened.

Lucy caught herself feeling faint from her whirlwind thoughts. "Sam is back. And what did Henry say? How did he know about my scar?"

She didn't realize Mrs. DeWitt had been standing there until then. Lucy turned to look at her.

"Lucy," Mrs. DeWitt said as she reached out and took Lucy's hand, "what happened? You're shaking."

Lucy looked down to see her hand shaking in Mrs. DeWitt's hold. "I-I-I...Sam's back," she finally got out.

Chapter Nineteen

"Oh dear," Mrs. DeWitt said, pulling Lucy into a hug. "Well, don't you worry. We won't let him anywhere near you."

Lucy was grateful for Mrs. DeWitt's mothering since Lucy had told them how she got the scar, but that made her wonder.

"Mrs. DeWitt," she said as she pulled out of the embrace, "forgive me if this sounds rude, but you didn't tell anyone how I got my scar, did you?"

"Heavens no! Why would I do that?"

"I didn't think you would. It's just...Henry seems to know."

"Henry?"

"The man that was at the counter. He's Sam's brother." Lucy shivered at that fact.

Mrs. DeWitt reached out to her again. "Maybe that's how he knows, then? Maybe Sam told him."

Anything was possible where Sam was concerned.

"Maybe," Lucy said, trying to convince herself.

"Let's go to the back and make you some tea. I think you could use the break. William," Mrs. DeWitt called out to her husband, "we'll be in the back room for a bit."

4

Henry and Sam didn't utter a single word to each other almost the entire way to Sam's place. Henry preferred it that way. He was not just angry at Sam for the way he had left Beth and the boy now. He was angry for him just blowing back into town like nothing had happened. More than anything, though, he was angry at him for speaking to Lucy. He didn't want his filthy brother anywhere near her.

"So, are you seeing that girl in the mercantile?" Sam asked, breaking the silence.

"You're going to leave her alone, Sam," Henry said.

"Am I?" Sam asked, snorting. "Why would I want to do that?"

"You've caused enough trouble where she's concerned."

"What? I haven't gone near her."

Henry remembered Matthew saying Sam was drunk that day. Maybe he didn't remember hurting Lucy, but it didn't matter. Henry would make sure he stayed away from her.

They pulled into Sam and Beth's yard.

Sam whistled. "Man, Beth's doing a pretty good job keeping the place in shape. I don't know what all the fuss was about. She can obviously handle things here without me." Sam jumped out of the wagon and grabbed his bag from under the seat. "I wasted money coming here, it seems."

Henry came around the wagon, squared up in front of his big brother, and leaned into him. "The only reason this place looks decent is because I've been here for over a month putting everything back together for your family. I should be home taking care of mine, but instead, I'm cleaning up after you."

Sam started to say something, but Henry stopped him.

"Before you try to claim any glory for this place, I want you to know something. I tried to get Beth to divorce you, but she won't. She's a good woman. She doesn't deserve a man like you for a husband, and Sammy sure as hell doesn't deserve not having his father around. They didn't ask for any of this. You did this to them. You moved them out here and then left them for gold you've never found and women that don't want to be tamed. Do them both a favor. Cut the ties and let them be."

Sam tried to say something again.

"Save it. We both know what you're about to say is a lie, and I really don't want to hear it right now," Henry said.

He walked around Sam and started gathering supplies from the wagon, then walked to the barn, leaving Sam standing there alone, at the place he once called home.

It was a small, simple structure made with logs. There was nothing glamorous about it—not like the hotel he'd been living in back in San Francisco. The area surrounding the house was nothing special—just dirt, animals, and a garden. He hated the disgusting smell of that place. It made a man like him unable to breathe.

He knew when he moved Beth and the boy there that he wouldn't be able to stay. He did try, though, to earn an honest living raising cattle and giving his family a stable place to live. He'd lasted all of five months before he started venturing into town to drink, gamble, and spend some time with a woman who understood him.

He knew Beth wasn't a fool. He didn't know if she knew everything, but she had some idea what he was doing, and he thought he'd seen relief in her eyes the last time he rode away. Maybe that was just his imagination trying to justify leaving, though. He knew he didn't intend to come back.

Sam was surprised by Henry's last telegram. He couldn't let Beth divorce him. Although it would set him free to live as he wanted, he didn't want to be known as a man who couldn't keep a woman, so he got back as fast as he could.

He didn't intend for Ann to come with him, but she was a feisty one and you didn't dare tell her no! It would create a problem for him if she didn't stay put in the hotel, though. The real question was if he cared.

❧

Beth watched the two men from inside the house. She couldn't believe Sam actually had the nerve to come back there. In her heart, she wanted to believe he came back because he loved her and Sammy, but she knew better. Those telegrams from Henry had made him crawl back.

Beth heard Sammy yelling outside. She stepped closer to the window and watched as Sammy went running into his father's arms.

Tears formed in her eyes. "He's the innocent one in all this," she thought, praying that Sam wouldn't break their son's heart again.

❧

Chapter Twenty

Lucy sat at the simple wood table in her room above the store. Sketching always soothed her nerves, and she still hadn't quite recovered from the events earlier in the day.

She found herself sketching Henry's face. He'd never looked so intense before, and he'd appeared to have wanted to protect her from Sam. It had shocked her when Henry touched her scar.

Her mind lingered on the memory. "Did he want to kiss me?" she wondered.

While Lucy was curious, she was thankful for Mrs. DeWitt's interruption. Too much had happened at once, and Lucy couldn't process it all at the time. She thought about the motherly way Mrs. DeWitt had taken care of her after Henry and Sam had left—sitting with her in the small storage room, drinking tea, and speaking calmly to her.

Lucy appreciated the way Mrs. DeWitt took care of her. She was starting to like this woman and felt slightly ashamed for using her. Lucy's mother had passed away a few months before she made the trip out to Rock Springs.

Lucy shook her head. She needed to stay focused on her plan. She'd been working at the mercantile long enough most people were used to seeing her there now. She had started sitting with the DeWitts at church on Sundays, and although the women in Mrs. DeWitt's circle still talked down to her, they were friendly most of the time. Maybe now was a good time to move on to the next step in her plan.

She looked down at her drawing of Henry. She had captured that look in his eyes very well. She picked up the sketch, took off the cover to her kerosene lamp, and lit it on fire. She put it in an empty bowl on the table and watched it burn, telling herself she was burning any chance of a life with him along with it.

&

Henry tried to focus on the task in front of him. The barn just needed a few more repairs, but if he thought Sam was going to help him, he was mistaken.

During breakfast, Sam acted as though he had every intention of helping but then he ran off with Sammy to the creek that ran behind the property.

Henry wasn't upset with Sam for not helping him though. He was upset with him just for being there, but he didn't understand why. Henry had a child of his own he needed to get back to. But after yesterday, he knew he couldn't go just yet.

❧

It was suppertime when Henry hammered the final nail in place on the barn's last repair. He was tired and sore from spending the whole day working on it alone, and he was no closer to understanding why he felt conflicted the way he did. He was not a man who didn't know his own mind.

He wanted Beth and Sammy to be happy and taken care of because they were his brother's family. Deep down, he wanted his brother to take responsibility and stop counting on others to clean up his messes.

"Of course, if we would all stop cleaning up after him, he wouldn't be able to count on us, would he?" Henry thought.

That realization bothered him. Henry had looked up to Sam when they were little. He had thought his big brother was the master of mischief because Sam was always able to talk his way out of getting into trouble—until he discovered the poker table and the whiskey that went with it.

Sam started pulling all-nighters at the saloon when it first opened in their hometown. Once, he took Henry along against their parents' wishes. Henry wasn't into the card game and couldn't stand the taste of whiskey then. He was only fifteen. He sat and watched his brother get drunker and drunker that night and turn into a completely different person.

Sam didn't seem to remember much about that night, but Henry remembered every detail. That was the first time Sam struck a woman.

The saloon girl that had been "entertaining" their table had been very friendly, and Sam had taken a liking to her and had her sit in his lap. After winning a few hands, he declared her his good luck charm. She had other tables to take care of, but Sam wouldn't let go of her. She tried, in the most polite way she could, to explain that she needed to take care of the other tables, but in his drunken state, he refused to listen. He stood and backhanded her across her face, demanding that his table was the only one she needed to be concerned with. Then he sat back down and took her with him.

The saloon keeper saw Sam hit the girl and came over, took her off his lap, and kicked both Sam and Henry out. Henry never went back, but Sam managed to slither his way back in.

There were rumors after the incident that Sam still occasionally took his hand to a woman. Henry figured they were true because Sam usually hung around the house more after an episode at the saloon. He never took the blame though. It was always the girl's fault somehow.

Sam had met Beth at the saloon. She had started working there shortly after arriving in town. Somehow, they became a couple, and in a few short months, Beth was pregnant with Sammy.

Their wedding was small and simple, held after Sunday morning service. They said their "I do's" and headed off toward Rock Springs, where no one would know them and they wouldn't have to hide the pregnancy.

"Maybe that was why Beth stayed," Henry thought. Maybe she was ashamed of the whole relationship and couldn't bear admitting her mistake.

Henry put the tools away and made his way to his brother's house. He didn't want to clean up his brother's messes anymore, and he wasn't going to force Beth to do something she didn't want to do. No, they could both take care of their own problems. Henry was done helping them.

❧

Chapter Twenty-One

When Henry lay down that night, he knew he had to make sure Lucy was okay. He saw how Sam's eyes flickered when he'd seen her in the mercantile. Sam always got that look when a woman intrigued him.

Most women responded back in a flirtatious way, but Lucy had a look of pure fear on her face. Henry couldn't risk his brother hurting her again. He had to stay, at least until he figured out what Sam was up to.

Henry rolled onto his side, closed his eyes, and thought of Lucy, going over every inch of her face in his mind. He felt the softness of her hand under his when he touched her and remembered how small she was against him when he had found her crying in the alley. As he lay there thinking about her, all he wanted to do was take care of her—love her as fully as she deserved.

Sunday morning, Lucy sat next to Mrs. DeWitt as she waited for church to start. Mrs. Greyson was turned around talking to Mrs. DeWitt when she looked toward the back door and gasped. Mrs. DeWitt and Lucy whirled around to see what was the matter.

Lucy's hands began to shake as she watched Henry, Sam, a woman, and a small boy walk in. Mrs. DeWitt grabbed Lucy's hand and smoothed her thumb over it, trying to calm her.

She leaned toward Lucy. "What's he doing here?" Mrs. DeWitt asked.

"I-I-I don't know," Lucy stammered.

Mrs. DeWitt placed her other hand on top of Lucy's and said softly, "Don't be afraid, dear. He's not going to hurt you again. I won't let him."

Lucy looked at Mrs. DeWitt and knew she meant it. Lucy tried to smile but looked down instead. She heard them shuffle into the row behind her. She wondered where Henry was in the row but didn't want to turn around for fear of making eye contact with Sam.

"I can't see, Uncle Henry," she heard the little boy say.

"Here, you can sit on my lap, but you have to be still," Henry said, adjusting himself right behind Lucy.

Lucy's cheeks flushed. She didn't know which was worse, Sam in church or Henry right behind her, watching her every move.

Henry couldn't concentrate on anything Pastor Tom said. Sam had surprised all of them when he announced they would be attending church this morning. Henry had tried to decline but Sam insisted he go, and something in Sam's tone had suggested he not argue with his brother.

He couldn't help but watch as Lucy fidgeted in her seat. He had seen her cheeks redden just a bit when they shuffled into the pew. She never turned around to greet them, but the woman beside her had turned briefly and then faced the front again.

Pastor Tom was muttering something about "do unto others." Sammy turned his head into Henry's shoulder and closed his eyes. Sam had kept the little boy up late the night before, telling him stories about the places he had been despite Beth trying to get Sammy in bed.

Henry still hadn't figured out why Sam was back. The telegrams had something to do with it, but Henry wasn't convinced there wasn't more to it.

Henry noticed that Pastor Tom looked at Sam a lot as he preached. Was Pastor Tom trying to save his eternally condemned brother? He doubted it. Anyone who knew Sam knew he couldn't be saved.

❧

Pastor Tom tried not to look at Sam, but he couldn't help himself. He would have to find a way to talk to Sam—to find out why the vermin came back and exactly what he was up to—because as far as he knew, he was the only person that could destroy him.

❧

Sam sat in the church pew, smiling inwardly. "The shock on good ole Pastor Tom's face when he saw me was worth dragging my worthless family to church," he thought.

It felt good to be back in town, but Sam knew his visit would be short. He wouldn't be back at all if it hadn't been for his meddling brother.

Sam glanced sideways at Henry. Hatred poured over Sam as he watched his son all snuggled up in Henry's lap. Henry had always been the good man, the good son. Now here he was being the good uncle and the better father to Sammy.

"How dare he come here and clean up my supposed mess!" Sam thought. "It wasn't a mess until Henry intervened."

Sam had tried to ignore all those annoying telegrams from Henry and their father. Why couldn't they just leave him alone, let him be? He was quite happy living the single man's life in San Francisco. He sent money when he had a little to spare, which wasn't often due to gambling debts and hotel bills.

He'd been kicked out of just about every saloon and hotel there. That was one of the reasons he was back. He had to let things cool down some in California. There were too many people there looking for him to collect their debts.

Another reason he hightailed it back, though, was that telegram threatening divorce. No woman was going to divorce him if he had anything to say about it.

"Divorce! Who'd heard of such a thing?" Sam had thought. "No woman ups and ends a marriage. It doesn't matter if they lived together or not."

From what he could tell, the telegram about divorce was all smoke. Beth was being the ever-attentive wife and mother. Henry must have threatened it to get Sam's attention.

Sam had planned to go to a nearby town for a while—just until things died down—but then he received another telegram as he was leaving the hotel. It seemed Mark didn't like having Henry in town any more than Sam liked having his little brother at his house doing his job as husband and father. Mark had written that Henry and that pretty little Lucy were up to something that wouldn't do any good for Mark's high social standing in town, so Sam decided that a few hundred miles was a good distance to put between him and John Wilson, the brother of the man he had cheated out of money and life, in order to help Mark.

Sam's cockiness always seemed to get him in trouble with the men he cheated. If he could keep his mouth shut and just cheat, he would have been fine to stay, but Sam was never one to miss an opportunity to let a man know what a fool he was. Unfortunately for John Wilson, drawing his gun on Sam in defense of his money lost him his life.

Being back on the ranch made Sam antsy, but he enjoyed the times he could get Sammy away from helping Henry or Beth. They would go down to the creek and Sammy would fish while Sam took a nap propped up against a tree.

Sam liked Sammy. Always had. He didn't know if he loved him, though. Sam just never had any desire to be a father.

He remembered when Beth had told him she was pregnant. He accused her that night of being with someone else, but he knew she hadn't been. He was the one that wasn't faithful. He had told her that while he felt bad for her, he couldn't help her.

Sam had never seen Beth's anger before that night. She told him he would marry her or the whole town would know all his dirty little secrets, so he did and then moved the two of them off to Rock Springs so they could start fresh.

Sam had hoped that if they were away from all the people they knew he would learn to love Beth, but he had been a fool. Once he discovered the saloon there, he knew his true love was the whiskey and cards within those four walls.

Life had been good up until the day he had slapped that girl. He pretended not to remember her in the mercantile, but he knew full well who she was. He didn't need to see the scar from the bureau.

He had watched Henry with her for a little bit before he spoke up to let them know he was there. Henry liked the girl. It was plain as day. Too bad Sam was going to have to ruin that for him.

Sam sat back against the pew and waited for Tom to finish spewing his biblical mumbo jumbo. He knew better than anybody just how much their beloved pastor lived contrary to the words he spoke every Sunday. He couldn't wait for church to be over. He felt like playing cards and he needed to see Ann if she was still there.

She had been a good distraction when Sam experienced moral moments that whispered, "Go home." Anytime he started thinking he needed to return to Beth and Sammy and be the good husband and father they needed, Ann would sashay in and help him lower his standards back down, which is where he preferred to live. Sam hoped she was still in town.

❧

Chapter Twenty-Two

Lucy had seen Melissa come in and sit two rows in front of her. Lucy wondered how she was doing. Melissa was part of the reason Lucy had changed jobs and where she lived. Lucy had thought she had a lesson to teach this town, but now she was feeling guilty. Melissa was her best friend, and she hadn't been by to see her in a month. Maybe she could remedy that this afternoon.

Lucy stood outside the church watching for Melissa. Mark had come out before her and was now talking to Sam. They seemed to be friends. That didn't surprise Lucy. They were both scoundrels.

When Lucy saw Melissa, she walked over to her. "Hey, Melissa," Lucy said. "How have you been?"

Melissa glanced in Mark's direction. "I've been fine."

"I'm sorry it's been so long since I've been out to visit," Lucy said. "There's been a lot going on."

Melissa looked at Lucy. "I heard you are working at the mercantile now."

"Yes, I needed to leave the saloon. It wasn't a good place for me to be anymore."

Lucy didn't want to go into detail while standing out in front of the church. She wanted to tell her best friend everything that had happened, everything she was working on.

"Maybe I'll come out and see you this week," Lucy suggested.

"I don't know if that's such a good idea. Mark doesn't really like for me to have company. He says it distracts me from my duties with the kids and him."

Lucy saw it then. The Melissa she had known was gone. The woman before her now was just a shell. Mark had beaten Melissa down to nothing. Her hair was pulled back, and Lucy could see clearly how sunken her cheeks were. She looked down at Melissa's hands that had been twisting against each other as she spoke. They were bone thin, bruised, and reddened. She also noticed Melissa was slightly stooped as she stood there. She used to be taller than Lucy when she stood at her full height.

Rage burned inside Lucy. She was angry she had gotten so caught up in what she was doing that she had neglected to check on her best friend regularly, and she was furious with Mark for beating the life out of Melissa. Lucy had never known herself to hate anyone, but she hated him.

Lucy looked at Mark standing there chatting with Sam. The sight of both men made her sick. Neither was worth the air he was breathing.

❧

Mark looked over at Lucy talking to Melissa. He said something to Sam and then walked toward them.

"Melissa, I'm staying in town this afternoon. You round up the kids and go home."

"Yes, sir." Melissa said.

Lucy was in shock. Melissa didn't even try to argue. She just did as she was told.

As she went to get the kids, Mark barked more orders at her. "Make sure you get all the chores done before I'm home, Melissa."

She turned and asked, "When will that be?"

"When I feel like coming home," he growled. "Just do as you're told and get things done. I don't want to find out that you slacked off again, you hear me?"

Melissa put her head down and walked off without even saying bye to Lucy.

Mark turned to Lucy then and put his finger in her face. "And you stay the hell away from her. She's doing just fine and doesn't need you interfering, you understand me?"

"That's not a nice way to talk to a lady."

Henry was standing behind Lucy. She wasn't sure when he had shown up.

"You stay out this," Mark said.

"Apologize for speaking to Lucy like that and I will."

"I'll do no such thing. This little tramp has a habit of putting her nose where it don't—"

Henry was in front of Mark before he could finish his thought. He was taller than Mark by a good two inches.

"I told you to apologize to Lucy. Now do it," Henry said.

Henry thought Mark was going to try to smart off again. Instead, Mark looked at Lucy and mumbled a quick apology before running back over to Sam.

"You didn't have to do that," Lucy said.

Henry looked her. He wanted to reach out and touch her somehow but knew he couldn't with Sam nearby. "He needed to be put in his place," Henry said.

Lucy just looked at him.

Henry wondered what she was thinking. Her big blue eyes staring up into his drove him crazy.

"Some men don't know how to properly treat a woman. I hope you have a good afternoon," he said and lifted his hat to her before walking over to Beth and Sammy.

"Are you ready to go home?" Henry asked.

They both nodded and headed toward the wagon. As Henry got on his horse, Sam came over to them.

"I'm staying in town this afternoon, maybe for the night," Sam told them.

"I don't think that's a good idea," Henry said.

"Doesn't matter what you think. That's what I'm doing," Sam said and walked off.

Henry looked at Beth and then at Sammy. Sammy's little face was scrunched up trying to figure out what was happening.

Henry looked back at Beth and just shook his head. "Some things never change," he said and urged his horse forward.

❧

Lucy spent the afternoon in her room above the mercantile. She paced the room waiting for water to boil in her kettle while trying to sort out everything that had transpired outside the church earlier.

First, she thought about Melissa. She had looked so fragile. Her face was sunken in and her waist was hardly visible. Lucy wondered what all Mark had her doing as far as "chores" went and if Melissa was eating properly.

Lucy remembered how Melissa winced as Mark barked his orders at her. "Is Melissa afraid of him now?" Lucy wondered.

The way he treated Melissa was despicable and when she thought of him and Sam palling around together this afternoon, it sent chills up her spine. "Those two men are evil when they are alone. I can't imagine how bad they are together," Lucy muttered.

She thought about how Mark had spoken to her and how surprised she was to hear Henry's voice behind her. Lucy wasn't sure how she felt about him standing up for her. The only other person ever to do that was Matthew—when Sam had hit her—and she wasn't sure why Henry had. Short of the almost kiss on the cheek in the mercantile, there was nothing between them.

Lucy absently reached up and touched her scar as she thought about the tender way Henry had been with her that day, then shook the thought out of her head as the feel of the scar beneath her fingers brought back her shame.

The kettle whistled and Lucy poured the hot water over some chamomile tea leaves in her teacup, trying to remember what was said that day. She put the kettle back of stove, took her teacup to the table, and sat down.

She closed her eyes while her tea steeped and remembered how Sam had looked at her in the store. She knew he remembered her. He had a slight smile tugging at the corner of his lips, like he was enjoying rousing her and Henry.

Lucy picked up her spoon and gently stirred her tea. Henry had looked like he was angry with Sam. Lucy thought it was because Sam hadn't waited outside. That's what Henry said, wasn't it? Then she remembered what Henry had said to her just before he left. He told her he wouldn't let Sam hurt her again.

"He knew!" she realized. "But how? Who told him? Surely not Sam, or would he have boasted to Henry about it?"

Henry didn't seem happy when Sam was around. She had watched him with Sam after he had spoken to Mark. Henry didn't appear to be okay with whatever Sam told them. That made Lucy believe Sam wasn't the one who told Henry what had happened.

Lucy drifted back to that day in the mercantile. As soon as Sam was out of sight, Henry had softened and spoken gently to her, just as he had when he found her in the alley. His eyes were soft when he looked at her, like he cared for her.

She raised her hand to her cheek where his hand had lingered briefly and took a deep breath as she remembered how he had been with her. She was okay with him knowing about what happened. For some reason, it mattered that he knew. She didn't care who told him. All that mattered was he still cared about her. Lucy couldn't wait to see him again.

Chapter Twenty-Three

Matthew didn't like what he saw as the saloon doors swung open. "I thought I told you, you weren't welcome here anymore," he bellowed toward the door.

Sam looked at him and smiled. "Now, Matthew, surely you can forgive a simple accident."

"My girl crashing into the side of a bureau as a result of your hand was no accident. Now get out of my place!"

"Matthew, don't be a fool," Mark said from behind Sam, his hand still on the saloon door. "I'm sure Sam didn't mean it. C'mon, Sam. Let's get a table."

Matthew watched as the two men went to a table in the corner away from the window. He saw Catherine heading toward them and stopped her.

"Catherine, tend the bar while I go serve those two some whiskey."

Matthew grabbed a bottle and two glasses and made his way over to them.

Sam looked up as he approached. "Now, no offense, Matthew, but you aren't the pretty lady I was hoping would wait on us."

Matthew slammed the glasses down, popped the top off the bottle, and poured the whiskey. Then he looked at Sam. "You're in my establishment. That means I decide who serves you, and no girl that works for me is going to come anywhere near you. That goes for you, too, Mark. You think there aren't any of us in town who don't know how you treat your wife."

Matthew picked up the bottle and put the top back on. "And you're a fool if you think I don't know what all you spend your time in town doing and who you're doing it with. Now enjoy your drink, fellas, because you're only getting this one glass. It's on the house. Then you can get the hell out of my place and never come back."

Matthew turned to go as the men tried to protest. "You heard what I said," Matthew spat, spinning back around to settle it once and for all. "You never should have touched one of my girls. Now drink up and get out. Oh, and be sure to pass all this along to your buddy, Tom. Tell him the back stairs is off limits to all of you."

❧

Henry decided to clean up some tools after lunch to keep his mind off going into town. He told himself it was because he needed to see what Sam was up to, but that was a lie. He wanted to see Lucy.

He didn't like the way that man had talked to her. Henry found out on the ride home who Mark was. Beth had told him all about how Mark had made a spectacle of his wife, Melissa, for being with another man.

Henry could understand Mark's anger over it, but Beth had also told Henry that Mark spent what hours he could in the saloon gambling, drinking, and enjoying the company of the girls that work there. And she had mentioned that Mark beat his wife.

Henry hadn't really noticed Melissa that morning, but he remembered the look on Lucy's face when he saw the two girls speaking to each other. And after the way Mark had spoken, first to Melissa and then to Lucy, Henry could believe what Beth said.

For the second time in four hours, Henry's body stiffened as he thought of how Mark was with Lucy. He didn't like it, not one bit. He could tell Lucy could hold her own when she wanted to from watching her back go rigid, not from fear, when Mark approached. She would not have backed down if Henry, who couldn't help himself, had not intervened. Henry didn't trust Sam or Mark, and those two being in town together didn't sit well with Henry at all.

&

Pastor Tom couldn't concentrate with Sam being back in town. He thought about riding out to their place to "check on the family."

He usually did his visiting throughout the week. All the ladies in the church loved to serve him, so it was a good way to get a meal without having to cook it himself. He had to endure their gossip, but it was worth it. He only half listened anyway unless something was interesting. That's how he found out about Mark beating Melissa nearly to death after catching her in the barn with Todd.

Mark was a loose cannon, just like Sam, but with Tom and Mark having similar interests, Tom had been sure he could keep Mark subdued—at least until he had confronted him about the beating.

Mark's threat to let Tom's precious congregation know just how bad of a sinner Tom was had been enough for Tom to go along with Mark humiliating Melissa. Tom hated doing it, especially in front of all those busybody women.

Tom had always thought Melissa was a beautiful girl. He didn't really know much about her, but he didn't think any woman deserved to be treated the way Mark treated her. Mark was incapable of loving anyone, and Tom didn't think anyone in town blamed Melissa for seeking comfort from someone else.

Tom needed to find Sam and Mark and figure out what they were up to. He knew those two fools together didn't add up to anything good.

❧

"Hey, Sam," Mark said as they slowly nursed their drinks, "what girl did you hit?"

Sam looked at Mark for a minute.

"Lucy."

Mark spit his whiskey out. "Lucy?"

"Yeah, why?"

"I was just curious." Mark thought about what he had just learned while he continued to drink.

Everyone was so worried because Sam was back, but it was Mark who was really the dangerous one. The things Sam had done were nothing compared to what Mark could and would do.

Mark smiled as he lifted his glass and said, "Let's finish this up, friend. I have a great idea."

❧

Chapter Twenty-Four

Henry felt antsy and couldn't concentrate. He fiddled with the ropes, then went to his horse and ran his hand along the beautiful chestnut creature's neck. He leaned his head against the front of the horse's head.

"You want to go for a ride, buddy?" Henry asked, rubbing the horse's nose. "I'm afraid Sam and his friend are up to no good, and I'm worried Lucy is in the line of fire."

"What the hell are you standing around here for, then?"

Beth's voice startled Henry. He looked toward the barn door.

"What?"

Beth walked toward him and the horse and placed her hand just behind the horse's right ear, caressing it.

"I saw how you looked at her today. I watched you try to protect her from Mark. You can't deny you like her," Beth said gently. "You don't hide it well."

Henry's eyes widened and Beth seemed to read his thoughts. "If I could tell, you know Sam saw it, too. If you're worried about her, go help her. Don't let Sam hurt her again."

"Again?" Henry asked. "You know, then, what he did to her?"

Beth nodded. "After Matthew threw him out of the saloon, he came home mumbling about what happened. He never said her name or fully told me what happened, but he left a couple of days after that."

"But, how did you know it was Lucy?"

"I put a few pieces together from his mumbling and then went into town after he left to inquire about the girl he hurt. I didn't talk to her. I spoke with Ms. Betty, and she assured me that Lucy was okay and recovering well."

"She has a scar from it."

"Henry, stop talking to me and go help your girl."

Henry looked at Beth for a minute and decided she was right. What could it hurt to check on her? He saddled up the horse and rode toward town.

❧

Tom headed toward the saloon, and Mark and Sam walked out just as he arrived. Tom gave

133

them a quick glance. They weren't drunk like they usually were after spending time there. They were standing upright and talking normal to each other instead of their usual wobbling through the street.

"Hey there, boys," Tom said.

Mark looked at Tom and smiled. "Hey, Tom, aren't you a little early?"

Tom ignored the remark. "I was looking for the two of you. Why don't we go back into the saloon and chat for a bit?"

Sam shook his head. "Nah, we can't do that. Matthew is still mad about the girl that got hurt."

Tom thought for a minute. "Well, how about you both come to my place? I'll make us some supper."

Mark was quick to agree to Tom's suggestion, so Tom turned and led the way, nervously wondering what Mark was up to.

❧

Henry rode up to the mercantile because he knew Lucy worked there, but it wasn't open on Sundays. He realized he wasn't sure what Lucy did on Sunday afternoons or even where she lived. Was she at her friend's place?

Henry got off his horse, secured the reigns to the post, and turned toward the saloon. Maybe Matthew would know where she was.

"Excuse me, sir?"

Henry turned around to the voice behind him. It belonged to an older woman who stood to her full height in a dress buttoned up to her neck.

"Can I help you, ma'am?" Henry asked.

"Actually, I think I can help you," she said.

Henry furrowed his brow. "I'm afraid I don't understand, ma'am, and I'm looking for someone right now."

"That's what I mean." The lady turned toward the store. "I'm Mrs. DeWitt. My husband and I own the mercantile. I saw you ride up. Are you looking for Lucy?"

Henry took in a quick breath at the sound of Lucy's name. "Yes, ma'am, I am. Do you know where she is?"

"She lives in the room above the store. I believe she went to her room after we all had lunch."

Henry wasn't sure what to do next. He wanted to run up the stairs to Lucy's room, but he held himself to the spot instead. He felt as though Mrs. DeWitt was waiting to see what he would do, and he didn't want to get Lucy into trouble.

"I would like to see her, if that's all right," Henry said.

Mrs. DeWitt squinted her eyes at him, and he could feel his cheeks redden as she decided what to do.

"You can wait in the parlor in my house next door. I'll let Lucy know you're here to see her."

"Thank you, ma'am," Henry said.

♪

Mrs. DeWitt walked up the stairs to Lucy's room and knocked softly on the door. When Lucy opened it, Mrs. DeWitt noticed dark smudges on her hands.

"Everything all right, dear?"

Lucy glanced down at her hands. "Oh, yes. I was just drawing." Lucy opened the door wider and stepped aside to let Mrs. DeWitt in.

"You draw?"

"Yes, ma'am," Lucy said, walking over to the table to clean up her mess.

Mrs. DeWitt picked up the sketch Lucy had been working on. It appeared to be the horizon to the west of town.

"Lucy, this is very good. How long have you been drawing?"

"I don't know. Since I can remember, I guess. It's very soothing." Lucy put away her pencils and things and went to the basin to clean her hands. "Did you need something, Mrs. DeWitt?"

"There's a young man waiting to see you in my parlor." She watched for Lucy's reaction. "I think it's the young man that has spoken to you in the store." Mrs. DeWitt saw Lucy's back stiffen and quickly added, "I think his name is Henry."

Lucy's back didn't relax with the knowledge that Henry was waiting for her. Instead, she grabbed the back of the closest chair. Her mind was spinning with questions. Why was he there? What did he want?

Mrs. DeWitt cleared her throat.

Lucy took a breath and turned to look at her. "What do you suppose he wants?"

"I don't know, Lucy. The only way you're going to find out is to go talk to him."

Together, the two women walked over to Mrs. DeWitt's house, where they found Henry being entertained by Mr. DeWitt.

🔥

Henry stopped talking when he saw Lucy enter the room. She was so beautiful, even with the hint of a dark smudge on her cheek. He let out a breath he didn't realize he had been holding, and his body relaxed as he took her in.

"Well, Mr. DeWitt and I will go put together a snack tray for you two while you talk," Mrs. DeWitt said as she started for the door. She looked at her husband, who didn't seem to take the hint. "Dear," she said as she grabbed his hand, "come help me make some snacks for our guests." She walked out with Mr. DeWitt reluctantly following behind.

❦

Lucy took a seat in one of the mahogany straight-backed chairs. Henry followed and sat in the one across from her.

"Mrs. DeWitt said you wanted to see me."

Henry stayed quiet for a minute. He didn't know how to tell her what he wanted to say. He looked at her, taking her in from the scar down to the place he had touched on her cheek as Lucy shifted in her chair.

"Henry," Lucy said, "what did you want to see me about?"

Henry straightened in his seat. "I just wanted to make sure you were okay after this morning."

Lucy scrunched her eyebrows together. "I'm fine. Why wouldn't I be?"

"I...it's...well, I just didn't like the way Mark spoke to you."

"Mark doesn't scare me."

Henry gave a short laugh. "I don't believe that! I don't trust him myself."

"But, does he scare you?" Lucy asked. "There's a difference between trust and fear."

Henry was shocked at Lucy's boldness. Maybe she wasn't scared of Mark, but he knew Sam was a different story.

"Well?" she asked again.

"No, he doesn't scare me. I just don't trust him, and I especially don't trust him and my brother together."

"What?"

"That's why I came into town, Lucy. Sam stayed in town with Mark after church, and I didn't want to chance something happening to you."

"Why would something happen to me, Henry? I stay away from them."

"That Mark is pure evil from what I've been told and I don't trust Sam for anything."

"Henry, I don't think they would come after me. I'm not a threat to them."

"You don't think so?" Henry asked. "I watched you today. You don't back down, and those two aren't the type of men that would take that well."

Boom!

The DeWitts house shook under their feet.

"What the—" Henry started to say.

Boom! Boom!

Instinctively, Henry grabbed Lucy and pulled her into him.

"What's going on?" she shrieked.

"I don't know."

❧

Chapter Twenty-Five

"Are you two okay?" Mr. DeWitt called, running into the parlor.

"Yes, we're fine," Henry said. "What happened?"

"I'm not exactly sure. Mrs. DeWitt had to let someone into the store. Maybe we'll find out when she gets back."

"There's smoke coming from the saloon," Lucy said, looking out the window and then pulling away from Henry and running out of the room.

"Lucy, where are you going?" Henry called, running after her.

"I need to go see if everyone is okay!" she yelled back.

Henry stopped when he saw the chaos outside Lucy was running toward. "Lucy, stay back!" he yelled but then realized she couldn't hear him as more people were coming out and yelling things at others.

Lucy stopped when she got to the saloon. Black smoke was climbing out of a hole in the roof. Large flames flicked out the windows on both floors, and people were running with buckets from the water pump line in the center of town to throw water on the burning building.

Off to the side, Lucy saw some of the girls from the saloon huddled together. As she got closer, she saw Matthew wasn't with them.

"Where's Matthew?" she cried.

"We don't know," Catherine answered. "Nobody's seen him since the first explosion."

Lucy looked around. "We have to find him."

She was about to make her way to the saloon when a hand on her arm stopped her. She looked up to see Henry.

"I have to find Matthew," she pleaded.

"No, Lucy," Henry said. "You can't go into the saloon. It's not safe. We'll look for Matthew as soon as we can."

She tried to pull away from his grip but he grabbed her and pulled her into his embrace, just as he had done in the DeWitt's parlor. Lucy could feel the strength in his arms as she tried to fight him.

"Henry, you're not listening…"

"No, Lucy, you're not listening. It's not safe for you to go into the saloon. We have to wait."

Lucy stopped fighting and started crying into his chest.

Henry relaxed his embrace and placed his cheek on top of her head. "It's okay, Lucy. We'll find him."

Boom!

Henry tried to keep them steady as the ground shook below them for a fourth time.

"Where did that come from?" someone yelled.

"The church," Lucy said, pulling away from Henry and turning toward the church. Henry kept his arm around her waist as he turned with her.

"What the hell is going on here?" he asked.

"I...I don't know." Lucy began to tremble as Henry pulled her close to him.

Several people ran to the church while others stayed to fight the fire in the saloon.

Henry wasn't sure what they should do. The only thing he was sure of was that he wasn't going to let Lucy out of his sight.

Henry had barely finished that thought when Lucy broke free from him.

"Matthew!" she yelled, running toward the alley Matthew was stumbling out from.

Henry ran over to them as Matthew collapsed. Being next to the saloon, they were too close to the fire.

"Here, let me get him up," Henry said as he put one arm across Matthew's back and lifted him up to his feet. "Can you walk?"

Matthew mumbled something Henry couldn't understand. Lucy stood got on Matthew's other side and together, they managed to get him into the street and far enough away from the fire.

Henry took a handkerchief from his pocket. "Lucy, go wet this down," he said. Then he squatted next to Matthew and asked, "What happened?"

Matthew shook his head. "I'm not sure. I was cleaning glasses behind the bar. I was the only downstairs. All the girls were upstairs, I think." Matthew scratched his head. "I was just cleaning a glass," he repeated, "and then the front window blew out and the next thing I knew, fire broke out everywhere."

Lucy came back, knelt beside them, and began wiping down Matthew's face.

Lucy watched as Henry gently tried to get Matthew to tell him what happened. He spoke softly, asking questions as Matthew told him what he could remember.

Lucy found Henry's gentleness breathtaking. She had only known men to be hard and sometimes cruel, including her own father on occasion. Lucy couldn't help but stare as she watched the two men interact.

Henry looked up at Lucy. He could feel her eyes on them and was afraid it would frighten Matthew. "Lucy, make sure you get his hands, too," he said to her, hoping to redirect her gaze. "Matthew, what happened right before the fire?" Henry asked. "Do you remember anything before the front window blew out?"

Matthew grabbed Lucy's hand to stop her from cleaning him up any further, then he looked at Henry. "I don't remember anything other than cleaning glasses," he said.

Henry patted Matthew's back and stood up. "Lucy, stay here with Matthew for a bit. I'm going to see what's happening at the church," he said, walking off before Lucy could protest.

He thought about what Matthew had said. It seemed strange that he wouldn't have heard something before the window blew out.

He glanced back to make sure Lucy had done as he had asked. When he saw her sitting beside Matthew, he continued toward the church. Henry had a feeling Sam was behind all of this somehow.

❧

The church fire appeared to be worse than the one at the saloon. Black smoke billowed above the steeple and flames flicked out doorways and windows. People were throwing water on it, but it didn't seem to help.

Henry was about to join the water line when someone yelled out, "She's coming down! Everyone get out of here!"

People ran from the church as it fell in on itself. There was no stopping this fire. The townspeople would take turns keeping watch until it burned itself out. The sheriff was amid the crowd trying to get some answers when Sam and Mark made their way from Pastor Tom's house.

"What's going on?" Mark asked.

"Can't you see?" Sheriff Daniel asked. "The church and saloon are on fire."

Mark looked at Sam. "Well, isn't that interesting?"

"Yeah, interesting," Sam said.

The sheriff groaned. "Look, either you two grab a bucket and help us out or get out of the way."

Mark threw his hands up. "Sorry, Sheriff. We'll be on our way.

Henry watched the two men walk off. He knew they were behind the fires. But why they had done it?

"Anybody seen the pastor?" someone asked.

Henry turned back to the crowd. People murmured among themselves. No one had seen the pastor.

Henry had an uneasy feeling, so he decided to check on Lucy and Matthew, who were right where he had left them. Lucy's eyes were wide, staring across the street. Henry followed her gaze and saw that the saloon, like the church, had collapsed and was still burning. Matthew was staring at the ground.

Henry knelt down before them. "How are you doing?" he asked them both.

Lucy stuttered, "Th-the saloon..."

"The saloon is gone," Matthew said, not lifting his eyes off the ground.

"Has anyone figured anything out yet?" Henry asked.

"I don't know," Lucy managed to answer. "We were just sitting here when the building fell."

Henry saw Mark and Sam in front of the mercantile. "Stay here," he said as he walked over to Mark and Sam.

He stood in the street in front of them and sized them up. They didn't appear to be drunk but were almost giddy—strange behavior for what the town was currently experiencing.

"What's going on, boys?" Henry asked as he moved closer to them.

Mark looked at him. Henry thought he was trying to hide a smile.

"Nothing, brother," Sam said. "Why don't you go home...back to Texas, where you belong?"

Henry squared his shoulders and clenched his fists. Sam appeared to be doing the same. Mark stepped between them.

"Now, boys, there's no need for bickering at a time like this," Mark said.

Henry unclenched his fist, noticing something behind where Mark had been standing. "Why is that door open?" he asked.

Sam and Mark turned toward the mercantile. "Hell, if I know," Sam said.

"Maybe they opened it for the afternoon given all that's happened," Mark suggested.

As Henry pushed the door opened, he noticed there was no one inside. He stepped into the store and saw a mess in the back corner. The air smelled of kerosene from broken lamps and overturned canisters.

He turned around to say something to Mark and Sam and realized they hadn't followed him in.

"Looks like someone broke into the store," he went outside and told them.

Just then, the sheriff came walking up with Mr. DeWitt.

"Martha probably forgot to lock it when she came out from getting Lucy earlier," Mr. DeWitt said.

"Yes, well, let's take a look and see what we find."

Henry spoke as they got closer. "The kerosene lamps and oil are a mess."

"What?" Mr. DeWitt asked, confused.

"I saw the door ajar, so I went in to make sure everything was okay," Henry explained. "I found the kerosene items all broken and toppled over."

The sheriff walked past Henry into the store. Mr. DeWitt and Henry followed. In the back corner, the sheriff knelt down to take a closer look. He glanced over his shoulder at Mr. DeWitt and asked, "Does it look like anything is missing here?"

Mr. DeWitt squinted his eyes and tried to take in the scene before him. "It's hard to tell, really," he said finally. "There's so much broken glass here, I don't know if anything was actually taken or just broken."

"Well, with the day's events, I think it's safe to assume someone broke in and took some kerosene," Sheriff Daniel said.

Mr. DeWitt walked to the back door and tested the door knob. It was locked. "Well, it looks like they only used the front door," he said.

As the men tried to figure out what might have been taken, they heard a muffled sound coming from behind the counter.

The sheriff stood up, drew his gun, and walked slowly to the counter.

"Mrs. DeWitt!" The sheriff holstered his gun and bent down to check on her as she came to on the floor.

"What!" Mr. DeWitt screamed, running over to his wife.

Henry joined them, and the sheriff propped Mrs. DeWitt up against the shelf. "We need to get her a cool cloth," he said.

Mr. DeWitt stood up and disappeared into the back room for a minute. Henry looked her over as best he could. He didn't see any bruises but noticed her rubbing the back of her head.

Mr. DeWitt returned with a cool cloth and handed it to his wife.

"Mrs. DeWitt, what happened?" the sheriff asked.

Chapter Twenty-Six

Mrs. DeWitt looked at the three men crowding her. Her head was spinning and she didn't like the attention she was getting.

"If you don't mind," she said, "could you all give me a little space?"

Mr. DeWitt and Henry stood and backed away. Sheriff Daniel shifted his weight away from her and said gently, "I understand this may be hard right now, but we need to know everything you remember."

Mrs. DeWitt took the cloth and patted her face. She closed her eyes to try to stop the spinning. "I was at home, putting a snack tray together in the kitchen." She opened her eyes and looked at her husband. "Mr. DeWitt was supposed to help me, but he had retired to the bedroom for a nap instead." She glared at her husband, who cleared his throat and looked away as she spoke.

Mrs. DeWitt looked at Henry and then back at the sheriff. "There was a knock at the door. Beatrice was gone for the day, so I went to answer it." Mrs. DeWitt winced and closed her eyes again.

"Who was at the door?" the sheriff prodded.

Mrs. DeWitt squeezed her eyes shut trying to remember. "It was Pastor Tom," she said. Keeping her eyes closed, she went on. "He said he was out of something that couldn't wait until tomorrow, so he wanted me to open the store for him." She opened her eyes and looked at the three men again.

"Do you remember what he said he needed?" the sheriff asked. "No. I don't think it was anything too terribly important because I tried to convince him that it could wait."

"Okay, what happened after that?"

"We walked over here and I unlocked the door. We both walked in toward the canned goods." She took in a breath. "That's what he needed. He said he needed a few things for a lunch he was expected to be at tomorrow. It didn't make sense to me, but what do I know?"

The men waited as Mrs. DeWitt drew a breath and thought for a minute.

"The next thing I knew, I was waking up behind the counter here."

"You don't remember anything else?" the sheriff asked.

Mrs. DeWitt shook her head. "No." She rubbed the back of her head and winced.

The sheriff leaned forward and looked at her head. "You've got a nice goose egg developing," he told her. "You sure you don't remember being hit?"

"No, sheriff. I've told you everything I can remember right now."

Mr. DeWitt cleared his throat again, came forward to help her up, and said, "Sheriff, I think my wife has had enough for now. I'm going to take her home."

❧

As the DeWitts left the store, Henry thought about what Mrs. DeWitt had said. He didn't remember hearing a knock while he was at their house. Then again, Lucy had his full attention, so he figured it was possible he missed hearing it.

Henry also thought it was strange that the pastor would insist on opening the store for canned goods. It was well-known that he survived off the meals provided to him by the townswomen. There were jagged pieces of the chaotic puzzle coming together, none of which made sense to Henry yet.

"I think I'm going to check on the saloon and the church," the sheriff said to Henry.

Sam was lighting a cigar as Henry and the sheriff walked out of the store. "What was so interesting in there?" he asked his brother.

153

"Nothing that concerns you, I'm sure," Henry said in a flat tone.

"Why don't I believe your faith in me, baby brother?"

Henry ignored Sam's statement and walked off. He wanted to know what the sheriff would find at the burned buildings, but first, he went to check on Lucy and Matthew again.

They were still sitting where he had left them.

"Lucy, why don't you go help Mr. DeWitt with his wife?" he said.

Lucy gave him a confused look. "What's wrong with Mrs. DeWitt?"

"Someone hit her in the store," he explained. "She was knocked unconscious."

"What?" Lucy stood up quickly. "What happened? When was she in the store?"

Henry grabbed her arm as she stood up. He took her opposite hand in his and looked at her. "It's kind of complicated. I'll explain it to you later," he said.

"What about Matthew?" Lucy asked.

Matthew stood up when he heard his name. "I'm fine," Matthew said. "I'm going to try to find the girls and Ms. Betty." He gave Lucy a quick hug. "Thanks for taking care of me. Do as Henry said and go help tend to Mrs. DeWitt."

Henry and Lucy watched as Matthew walked away. "I'm worried about him," Lucy said.

"He'll be okay," Henry told her. "He needs to process all of this in his own way. Let's get you to the DeWitts' place."

"Henry, you don't have to walk me. I know where it is. I can get there on my own."

Henry inhaled deeply. Lucy still didn't understand how much he worried about her with Sam and Mark being together.

He put his hand under her arm to guide her. "It's on the way to the church anyway," he said.

❧

Lucy sat in the chair beside the DeWitts' bed, watching Mrs. DeWitt sleep. Mr. DeWitt was trying to rest in the parlor. Lucy leaned her head back against the chair, closed her eyes, and tried to think about everything that had happened since church let out.

Henry seemed to be very concerned about her wellbeing after witnessing her conversation with Mark. It baffled Lucy that he felt the need to ride back into town to check on her. At the same time, though, she thought it was sweet of him. Maybe he did care for her.

❧

Chapter Twenty-Seven

Lucy's thoughts turned to the other events of the day. She didn't understand why the fires had happened. Mr. DeWitt told her about what appeared to have happened at the store.

"Poor Mrs. DeWitt," Lucy thought. She wondered why Pastor Tom had insisted on her opening the store. "Surely he didn't have something to do with the fires." Then again, that wouldn't surprise Lucy with what she knew about him.

Lucy remembered seeing Sam and Mark in the street amidst the chaos. They weren't running like everyone else. No, they appeared to be on more of a leisurely stroll. She had thought that was odd at the time, but nothing those two did surprised her. She had just assumed they were being their usual, annoying selves. Now, though, she wondered what part those two played in what had happened.

"Lucy." Lucy opened her eyes and looked at the bed. Mrs. DeWitt was awake and talking to her.

"Lucy, what are you doing here?"

"I came to sit with you for a bit while Mr. DeWitt rested in the parlor." Mrs. DeWitt tried to sit up. Lucy quickly went to her and helped ease her up, propping pillows behind her.

"Humph! He acts like it was him that was hit today," Mrs. DeWitt said in disgust.

"I'm sure we are all in a bit of shock right now," Lucy suggested.

"Shock! Sure, but other husbands would be more attentive to their injured wives." Mrs. DeWitt winced as she spoke. "Oh, my head won't stop hurting."

"Here." Lucy rang out the rag that had been sitting in the basin of cold water, placed it on the back of Mrs. DeWitt's head, and eased her back onto the pillow.

"Oh, dear child, I'm sorry about being ugly," Mrs. DeWitt said. "It just hurts, and I can't remember how it happened. I've tried, but I can't seem to recall the time from walking over to the canned goods with the pastor to waking up behind the counter."

Lucy put her hand on the older woman's shoulder and said, "It's okay, Mrs. DeWitt. A lot has happened today. I'm sure there are plenty of questions left to be answered. Close your eyes and rest now. I'll go make us all something for supper."

Mrs. DeWitt placed her hand over Lucy's. "You are a dear, Lucy. Don't ever let anyone tell you different."

She patted Lucy's hand and closed her eyes. Lucy tiptoed out of the room, closed the door, and went into the kitchen. She put wood into the cast-iron stove so she could boil water for coffee and found food leftover from lunch. She decided that would work.

❧

The fire in the church had finally died down by the time Henry got back to it. Townspeople had continued to throw water on it in hopes of putting it out after the building collapsed. The burned timber smoldered in the early evening air. Sunset wasn't far away. Henry saw the sheriff talking to a few men and started to walk over to him when he heard a loud scream.

A woman was facing the church, hunched over and screaming at the top of her lungs. Henry and some others rushed over to ask what was wrong and console and calm her down. Nothing worked. She stared straight ahead at the church and screamed. Finally, she pointed toward the doorway.

Henry was the first to follow the woman's finger. There, in the doorway, lay a person on his side. Henry ran over to the body and slightly turned it to see the face more clearly. It was Pastor Tom.

He stood as others approached and tried to discourage the women from coming closer. Sheriff Daniel came and stood next to him.

"It's the pastor," Henry told him.

"I had a feeling," the sheriff said.

As people began to realize who the dead man was, questions started being shouted at the sheriff. They were upset and angry, the day's events catching up with all of them.

The sheriff turned toward Henry. "We've got to get these people away from the body," he said.

Sheriff Daniel raised his hands and whistled. Everyone stopped talking. He walked away from the church to push the crowd back. Henry followed him. Once the sheriff felt they were far enough away, he stopped and addressed the crowd around him.

"Okay, folks. It's been a hel'va day."

The people murmured in agreement.

"Our town has been hit hard today with, what is now three horrific events," he continued. "As the sheriff of our town, my job is to find out what happened today. I'm going to need everyone's cooperation as I try to figure this all out."

Again, the crowd murmured their agreement.

"I'm also going to need some volunteers to help me."

The sheriff paused, searching the crowd to see if anyone would offer himself to him. The crowd remained silent.

"Being that I now have a killing as well as two fires to solve, I'm going to choose a man and deputize him."

"Murder!" a man shouted. "You think the pastor was murdered?"

"I'm not sure, but nothing that happened today makes sense," the sheriff explained. He let that sink in before he spoke again. "As I was saying, I'm going to deputize one of you men to help me with the investigation."

The crowd remained silent as they waited to see who he would choose.

"I'm going to deputize Henry there." He pointed toward Henry.

"Wait a second, Sheriff," another man responded. "He's not from here. He can't be your deputy."

The crowd raised their voices in protest to Henry being deputy.

"I understand how you feel, Joe, but that is all the more reason for him to be my deputy," the sheriff tried to explain. "He should be able to be more fair not being from here."

"Ha!" a lady exclaimed. "Sheriff, don't you know who he is?"

The sheriff just looked at her.

"He's Sam's brother," she told him.

The sheriff looked at Henry for a minute. "That doesn't mean anything," Sheriff Daniel answered. "I've made my decision."

Something told him he'd made the right choice, but the crowd once again expressed their disapproval.

"Listen, I'm not going to argue with any of you," the sheriff hollered. The crowd quieted down, and the sheriff lowered his voice. "As I said, I've made my decision. Now please go back to your homes so we can see what we can determine before the sun goes down."

The crowd lingered for a few minutes, and Henry stepped back once the sheriff had made his announcement. Henry wasn't so sure he wanted to be deputized. He didn't blame people, either, for not wanting him to be a deputy. They didn't trust Sam. Why trust him?

Sheriff Daniel walked over to Henry. "So, I hope you're okay with my decision to make you my deputy," he said.

"Well, to tell you the truth, Sheriff, I'm not sure I'm the man for the job," Henry said.

"What makes you say that?" the sheriff asked.

"It's like the people said. I'm Sam's brother."

"So?" the sheriff said, still not understanding.

"No one is going to talk to me about today because of Sam, Sheriff," Henry said. "They don't trust me."

"I watched you today in the store, and I think you would be a great help to me with all of this," the sheriff said. "It doesn't matter who your brother is."

Henry took a deep breath. "If you say so, Sheriff. Where do you want to start?"

The sheriff smiled at Henry. "The body."

Lucy fed Mr. DeWitt and herself and managed to get Mrs. DeWitt to take a little broth and then she cleaned up the kitchen and checked on Mrs. DeWitt one last time before taking a walk. She wanted to see if the buildings were still burning, if anyone got hurt, and if they knew who did it.

When she stepped outside, Lucy saw the door to the mercantile open and walked over to see what was going on. The door creaked slightly as Lucy opened it and walked in. Mr. DeWitt was in the corner sweeping up glass.

"Mr. DeWitt, I can do that, if you would like," she said.

Mr. DeWitt stopped sweeping and looked up at her. "Lucy, I thought you were with Mrs. DeWitt."

"I checked on her before I left. She's sleeping right now," Lucy said.

"I don't know that I like the idea of leaving her alone," Mr. DeWitt said, "even if she's sleeping."

Lucy took in a deep breath. It wasn't like Mr. DeWitt to argue with anyone.

"Mr. DeWitt, I just stepped out for a minute," she said. "I didn't intend to be gone long, but I saw the door to the store was open and I came over to make sure everything was okay."

Mr. DeWitt was about to say something when voices came from the back of the store. Lucy recognized one of the voices as Henry's.

"What are they doing here?" she asked Mr. DeWitt as Henry and the sheriff walked in.

"They're trying to figure out what happened to Mrs. DeWitt and if this kerosene," he said as he swayed the broom toward the broken lamps, "had anything to do with the fires."

Henry saw Lucy standing next to Mr. DeWitt and sighed. He knew he couldn't force her to stay inside, but he wished she would understand how he wanted her to stay out of harm's way.

"Lucy, why aren't you with Mrs. DeWitt?" Henry asked.

Lucy narrowed her eyes at him. "Mrs. DeWitt is sleeping right now, and Mr. DeWitt needs help cleaning up this mess, if that's okay with you."

Henry put up his hands in defeat. "I just don't want to see you get hurt," he said, glancing at the top of her forehead.

Lucy placed her hand on her scar, stiffened her back, and stood a little taller. "I'll be just fine, thank you. Now, if you don't mind, I need to help clean this up."

"You know, Lucy," Mr. DeWitt said, "it wouldn't be a bad idea for you to stay at the house while Mrs. DeWitt recovers. I can stay in the room above the store."

Henry watched as Lucy tried to remain calm. Clearly, she didn't like being told what to do by either of them. He smiled as she squinted her eyes at him. "She sure is cute when she's mad!" he thought.

"I don't mind staying with Mrs. DeWitt, but she's sleeping right now. So, if it's okay with you two, I'm going to help with the cleanup here. When I am finished, I will walk back over to the DeWitts' house. Okay?"

Henry and Mr. DeWitt looked at each other. Henry laughed and said, "Okay, you win, Lucy. But please, don't go anywhere else without letting someone know."

"You mean without letting you know, don't you?" she asked.

Henry shrugged his shoulders. "Yes, I mean me," he admitted, walking toward the sheriff.

"She's a feisty one," Sheriff Daniel said.

"Yeah. What are you looking for over here?" Henry asked, not wanting to talk about Lucy with the sheriff. He didn't know him well and wasn't sure he could be trusted.

"This is where Mrs. DeWitt last remembers being before waking up behind the counter," the sheriff said. "She doesn't remember anyone with him, but I'm not sure the pastor had the ability to carry her over to where we found her without making a path of some sort."

Henry looked around. Nothing appeared to be disturbed between them and the counter. Nothing was knocked down or out of place.

"Sheriff, look over here," Henry said, walking toward the front of the store. He stopped just short of the counter and looked in the direction of the kerosene lamps. "There's bootprints."

The sheriff squatted down to get a closer look, then stood and followed their path.

"It looks like someone was over here getting the kerosene, then walked over to the canned goods and then towards the counter," the sheriff said. "The path gets lighter as it gets closer to the counter."

Henry looked at the path and tried to make sense of what the person had done. "How are we going to figure out who those boots belong to?" he asked.

"First, we need to take a closer look at the pastor's body. We'll check his boots against a tracing I'm going to make of one these prints."

The sheriff asked Mr. DeWitt for some paper and a pencil. Lucy looked up from collecting broken glass and glanced Henry's way. He wished she didn't drive him so crazy. He shifted his gaze when Lucy stood up and walked over to him.

"Henry," Lucy said as she approached.

"Yes, Lucy," Henry replied, trying to hide his agitation. He wanted her to go back to the DeWitts' house.

"Why are you helping the sheriff?" Lucy asked.

"The sheriff asked me to," Henry said. "He appointed me deputy to make it official."

Henry took the badge out of his pocket to show her, watching as Lucy eyed the badge. He wasn't comfortable wearing it for everyone to see.

"Why do you think he appointed you?" she asked.

"I don't know, but I know there are a few people who don't like it." Henry glanced at the small crowd gathering outside the store. "People have figured out I'm Sam's brother."

"So?" Lucy shrugged. "What's that got to do with you being a deputy and helping the sheriff?"

Henry took a good look at Lucy. In so many ways, she was a woman. Yet, in other ways, she was still an innocent girl. He glanced up at her scar. "I guess there are some people who think I'm just like him," he said.

"Well, I'll admit I wondered about you in the beginning. I know now, though, that you're nothing like him."

Henry smiled at Lucy's comment. "Thank you, Lucy."

"I think I got a good tracing of one of the prints," the sheriff said as he walked toward them. "Let's go take a look at the pastor's body," he said to Henry.

Henry watched Lucy shiver as he turned to leave. She placed a hand on his arm to stop him. "Henry, I know you mean well about wanting to keep me safe," she said, "but do me a favor…"

"What?" he asked.

"Look after yourself too."

Henry placed his hand on top of hers and squeezed it. "Don't worry about me," he said. "I'll be fine." He squeezed her hand again before letting go to catch up with the sheriff. He wanted to kiss her but fought the urge. Now was not the time.

☙

Henry stood with the sheriff, holding his breath and hoping they wouldn't be too much longer. The air still reeked from when the sheriff had ordered Dwain, the blacksmith, to take the lid off the pastor's coffin. At the first crack of the lid, Henry had rushed out the back to relieve himself of his noon meal.

"Yep, just as I thought. There were other people in the mercantile," the sheriff said, holding the boot tracing next to the boot on the dead pastor's foot.

"Okay, well, now that we know that, can we get out of here?" Henry asked.

"Not used to being around dead men, are ya?" the sheriff asked.

"No, it's not something I make a habit of."

"All right, let's go see Matthew," the sheriff said.

᛫

Mark spat on the ground as he watched Henry and the sheriff across the street. "They make an interesting twosome," he said.

Sam looked up from the rock he was toeing. "What makes you say that?"

"Well, I just find it funny that the sheriff chose your brother to help him."

Sam stared toward his brother for a minute. "Henry isn't anything to worry about," he said. "He probably got suckered into it. He doesn't like to get involved in other people's messes."

Mark looked at Sam and snorted. "Yeah, right. That's why he was living with your wife and son while you were gone."

Sam shoved Mark. "You leave my family out of it. That's my problem to deal with. Right now, we have other things to do."

Mark laughed. "Sure, whatever. Let's see where they go next."

᛫

Chapter Twenty-Eight

It had been a long, crazy day and Lucy was tired. Mrs. DeWitt was settled in for the night. Now Lucy wanted the same for herself.

She had just settled into bed when she heard the horse outside. Lucy was surprised to hear hoofbeats so late in the evening. She knew the sheriff had a few men watching the street, but the sound scared her all the same.

She pulled her robe out of the small suitcase she had brought, slipped it on, went to the front door, and cracked it opened. Lucy could see a figure getting off of a horse in front of the mercantile.

"Henry!" she called softly, watching him look up from the reins he was tying to the post. "Henry," she called again, a little louder.

He turned and walked toward her, and she walked out to meet him.

"What are you doing here so late?" she asked.

"I'm staying in town for a while. You shouldn't be out here," he said, putting his hand on her elbow and trying to direct her back into the house.

"Stop trying to tell me what to do, Henry," Lucy said as she jerked her elbow away.

Henry sighed. "Lucy, I'm just trying to protect you."

"I don't need protecting," Lucy said, narrowing her eyes at him.

"I'm not so sure about that," Henry admitted.

Lucy put her hands on her hips. "What do you mean by that, Henry?"

"Nothing. Go to bed."

Henry started to turn away, but Lucy grabbed his arm. "No!" she shouted. Then, realizing how loud she had been, she said more softly, through clenched teeth, "You will not say that and then try to dismiss me."

Henry stood there, staring at her. She could feel his eyes on her scar.

"Henry, talk to me," she said, shaking him.

Henry shook his head and took a deep breath. "I shouldn't have said anything. I'm probably wrong anyway."

"Wrong about what, Henry?" Lucy asked, watching as he looked at her scar again before he spoke.

"I think my brother is behind what happened today, and I don't want him to hurt you again."

Lucy loosened her grip on his arm. "Why do you care what happens to me?" she asked. "You don't know me."

"I know enough," Henry admitted, reaching up to touch her cheek.

Lucy closed her eyes at the feel of his hand on her face.

"Now, please go inside and go to sleep. I will see you in the morning," Henry said, leaning down and kissing her lightly on the lips. "Good night, Lucy. Please go inside now."

Stunned by the kiss, Lucy softly said, "Good night," then looked at him briefly and went inside.

As she turned to close the door, he said, "Thank you."

❧

Henry couldn't sleep. He kept thinking about Lucy, his brother, Charlotte, and what was happening in this town.

Henry thought about how nice it was to see Lucy before he had gone up to the room above the store. He smiled as he remembered her standing before him with her arms closed tightly in front of her to keep her robe closed. Even in anger, she showed modesty. Henry knew she couldn't have been a true saloon girl, and he was curious how she ended up here. She had a slight New England accent he wondered if she could still hear. He knew Charlotte would get a kick out of listening to Lucy talk.

Henry rolled onto his side slowly, hoping the cot wouldn't squeak too much and wake Mr. DeWitt. Henry's mind quickly flashed from Lucy and Charlotte to his lousy brother.

Henry and Sam were oil and water. Sam spent his life fighting for spoils, and Henry felt like his life was full of cleaning up his big brother's messes.

While Sam was no good, he had never intentionally killed someone as far as Henry knew. So, he wasn't convinced that the two fires and the pastor's death were entirely Sam's idea.

Henry had seen Sam and Mark watching his exchange with Lucy from an alleyway earlier. Something about Mark made Henry's skin crawl. He didn't care for any man that hit a woman, and he didn't have to overhear Lucy's conversation with Mark yesterday to know he was that type of man. His whole demeanor toward his wife and Lucy spoke for itself.

Henry wasn't really surprised to see Sam with Mark. In fact, he wasn't even disappointed in Sam.

He expected it. Henry had learned a long time ago that his brother had no interest in changing, not even for his son. It still baffled Henry that Beth was willing to stay with him.

Henry shifted in the cot again. One of the drawers in the bureau beside him caught his eye. It was slightly open and Henry could see what looked like sketches inside. Gently, he pulled the drawer open and took out the stack of paper. He propped up on one elbow and slowly went through the drawings of the town and countryside. There was one of the springs near Sam's place.

Henry smiled as he went through the stack. Lucy was very good at capturing fine details. He could see all the particulars of the items in the sketch of the store window, right down to the tiny labels.

Henry admired each one, amazed by Lucy's talent. But the sketch that surprised him the most was the one of him. Lucy had captured his image on paper. She had done a good job, too, showing every detail of his face, even the freckle on his left cheek.

Henry put the sketches back as he had found them in the drawer. He closed it and lay back down to sleep. He was still smiling as he closed his eyes and fell asleep to dream of Lucy.

At first, Lucy thought she was dreaming. She realized she wasn't when her bare foot hit the cold, hard floor.

She was being half dragged, half carried out of the bedroom. She tried to scream but couldn't. Someone's hand was on her mouth. Her eyes widened when she saw Sam trying to hold her feet up. She knew then it was Mark's hand on her mouth.

They were trying to take her out of the house, but Sam was having trouble getting the door open. He had to loosen his hold on Lucy's foot and when he did, Lucy kicked him as hard as she could. Before Mark could realize what was happening, Lucy bit him. She ran away from them, toward the steps to her room above the store, while they were dazed by what had just happened.

When she reached the first step, Mark caught up with her and pulled her down by her hair. Lucy screamed from the pain. With his hand still firmly wrapped around her hair, he yanked her back up to her feet. Lucy screamed again, and Mark backhanded her across her face.

"Get your hands off her!" Lucy heard someone yell as she tried to stay conscious. As blackness surrounded her, she heard a gunshot and wondered if she was the one dying as she fell to the ground.

"What the hell!" Mark hollered, ducking to the ground.

Henry ran down the stairs and tackled Mark, pinning him down and punching him. Lucy lay sprawled on the ground nearby, unconscious and motionless. Henry was afraid Mark had killed her.

Blow after blow, Henry got angrier and angrier. Lucy wasn't moving and Henry wanted Mark to pay for hurting her, but as he punched Mark, he realized he was looking at his brother.

Henry stopped for a second and looked down at his victim. He was hitting Sam. "How?" Henry wondered. "When did Sam appear and how did I mistake him for Mark?"

Henry looked over at Lucy again. Ms. Betty and Matthew were tending to her. Lucy was facing Henry with her eyes closed. Henry looked at her scar and then back at Sam. He punched his brother one more time, and this time, Sam, too, passed out.

❧

Chapter Twenty-Nine

"Henry!"

Henry got up off his brother and looked at Sheriff Daniel, who had appeared from nowhere. Mark was nowhere to be found.

"Where's Mark?" he asked.

"Mark wasn't here," the sheriff said.

"Yes, he was," Henry said. "I yelled at him to take his hands off Lucy right after he backhanded her."

Henry looked at Lucy. Matthew and Betty were still huddled over her.

The sheriff glanced in Lucy's direction. "You say Mark did that?"

"Yes, I ran down the stairs to stop him," Henry explained. "There was a gunshot as I ran down. I don't know what happened from there. I thought I was hitting Mark, not Sam."

The sheriff rubbed his jaw. "I see," he said. "The gunshot is what brought me down here." He looked at Henry. "You don't know where it came from?"

"It sounded like it came from across the street, but I'm not sure."

A muffled sound came from the ground. Henry turned to see Matthew and Betty helping Lucy sit up. Henry went over and knelt down in front of her, taking her hand as he did so.

"Lucy, are you all right?" Henry asked. She appeared to be dazed still as he waited for her to try to focus on him.

"What happened?" she asked.

Rather than answer, Henry looked at Ms. Betty. "Could you help her get over to the DeWitts' and tend to her there?"

"Sure," Ms. Betty said as she and Matthew helped Lucy to her feet.

Once Lucy was out of earshot, Henry spoke again. "I don't like what's going on here, Sheriff. I know I saw Mark hit Lucy, and I know someone fired a gun." He looked down at Sam on the ground and toed at him. "But where's Mark, and where's the gun?"

Sheriff Daniel scanned the area. "I say let's get this one over to the jail and wake him up. Maybe he can answer some questions for us," the sheriff said.

&

"Mrs. DeWitt, what are you doing out of bed?" Ms. Betty asked as they brought Lucy into the house.

"Oh, I needed to get out of that blasted thing," Mrs. DeWitt said. "Besides, who can rest with all that commotion outside?" Mrs. DeWitt watched as Matthew helped Lucy to a kitchen chair. "What happened to Lucy?" she asked.

"From what I gather," Matthew said as he straightened back up, "Mark hit her and knocked her to the ground."

"Oh, that poor child!" Mrs. DeWitt said.

"I think I got all the footprints, Martha," Mr. DeWitt said as he came into the kitchen carrying a mop.

"We have company, dear," Mrs. DeWitt said.

Mr. DeWitt took in the scene at the kitchen table. "What's going on here?" he asked.

"We think Mark attacked Lucy," Mrs. DeWitt said.

"He did attack me," Lucy finally said. "Him and Sam both."

❧

The group jumped at Lucy's sudden words. Mrs. DeWitt and Ms. Betty pulled out the chairs beside Lucy and sat down to face her.

"Tell us what you remember, dear," Mrs. DeWitt said.

Lucy looked at everyone. Her eyes rested on Mr. DeWitt for a minute. "What were you mopping up?" she asked.

Mr. DeWitt shrugged. "Just some bootprints that were all over the floor. Guess we had more company come to see Mrs. DeWitt than we realized."

"That wasn't company. That was Sam and Mark," Lucy told everyone. She took a deep breath and proceeded to tell them how they had dragged her from bed.

❧

Chapter Thirty

Henry scooped a ladle of water from the pail and carried it carefully into the cell that held his brother. Henry dumped the water on Sam's face.

"What the..." Sam said, sitting up.

"Oh look, Sheriff, Sam's awake," Henry called over his shoulder.

"Good," Sheriff Daniel said, getting up from his desk. "Maybe now we can get some answers."

"Answers?" Sam asked. "To what?"

"Don't play dumb, big brother," Henry said.

"Don't you tell me how to be!"

Sam shot up out the bed and flew at Henry.

"Why don't you tell the sheriff what you were doing, little brother?"

"Now, boys, arguing won't get us anywhere," the sheriff said, stepping between them before either brother threw a punch. "Henry, why don't you grab the chair by my desk and sit down?"

Henry moved the chair closer to the jail cell, and the sheriff closed the cell door, leaving Sam inside.

"Sheriff, why am I locked up?" Sam asked.

The sheriff went back to the chair behind his desk and sat down. "Boys, we have some things to figure out, so let's agree to be civil."

Sam humphed. "I'm not going to help you figure out a thing, Sheriff. I'm not about to help my perfect brother solve a crime and get the girl." Sam went over to the bed and lay back down. "No, I'm going to take this opportunity and take a nap. Try not to talk too loud now."

Henry stood up and moved his chair back to the desk. As he sat down, he said, "Don't mind Sam, Sheriff. He's never been good at actually helping people."

The sheriff rolled his eyes. "I don't know that I have ever seen two brothers be so different and so hateful toward each other," he said, looking over at Sam. "But then I'm sure it's hard being his brother. Now let's start from the beginning and see what we can figure out."

❧

"I don't understand why they were after you," Ms. Betty said after hearing Lucy's story.

"Those men are mean, hateful creatures," Mrs. DeWitt said, tilting her head. "They don't think of anyone but themselves."

"Fussing about them doesn't solve anything," Matthew finally said after remaining quiet as he listened to Lucy and the others.

Those two men were terrorizing the town bothered him, and he wanted it to stop. But short of killing them, he wasn't sure how to do it.

"Something needs to be done about those men," Mrs. DeWitt said.

"But what?" Lucy asked. "The sheriff has never been able to lock them up."

"Why would he lock us up?"

Everyone jumped at the sound of Mark's voice in the doorway.

"What the hell are you doing here?" Mr. DeWitt asked, dropping the mop.

Mark was holding his right side. Blood covered his fingers. "I've been shot," Mark said. "I need someone to dig the bullet out."

Mrs. DeWitt stood up.   "You won't get any help from us," she said, picking up the mop and thrusting the head at Mark. "Get out of my house!"

Mark cocked the pistol in his left hand. "Listen, woman," he said between clenched teeth, "one of you is digging this bullet out, and that's all there is to it. Now who's it going to be?"

"I'll do it." Matthew answered before anyone else could.

"Good. Glad to see there's a smart one in the bunch," Mark said, heading down the hallway to one of the bedrooms.

"No," Matthew said. "I'll take the bullet out, but I'll do it right here at the table."

Mark winced, knowing sitting up would be more painful than lying down, but he needed it out. He moved to the table and sat on top of it, and everyone scattered like mice when the lantern's lit.

❧

Chapter Thirty-One

After an hour of discussing the previous day's events, Sheriff Daniel decided they needed to walk all the crime scenes in chronological order.

"What about Sam?" Henry asked as they got up to leave.

The sheriff looked over at the cell. Sam seemed to be sleeping soundly. "We'll leave him in there for now," he said. "He'll have a harder time causing trouble."

"Yeow!" Mark hollered as Matthew dug into his side. "Don't you have any whiskey in this house?"

Mr. DeWitt moved to go to the parlor.

"We don't," Mrs. DeWitt said, looking at her husband. He stopped and turned back into the kitchen.

"Then give me a spoon to bite on, er, something," Mark pleaded.

"No!" Mrs. DeWitt demanded. "I refuse to give a man like you any comfort in my home. It's your fault you got shot. Bear the pain of it."

Everyone seemed stunned by her words.

Matthew continued to work on Mark, plunging the knife into his side again to try to dig the bullet out. Blood oozed out of Mark's side and he screamed in pain.

Like Mrs. DeWitt, Matthew didn't care if Mark suffered. He deserved it for all the pain and misery he had caused people over the years.

&

Henry and the sheriff stood in the street, staring at what was left of the saloon. Henry wanted answers but was unsure what he was supposed to do as a deputy, so he waited for the sheriff to do or say something.

Finally, the sheriff moved forward, toward where the window used to be. He took a quick look around before going inside.

Henry followed him. "What exactly are we looking for?" he asked.

"Something that is out of place," the sheriff said.

The sheriff moved slowly around the open area of the saloon, watching his step and taking his time looking around. Henry mimicked the sheriff's moves. It was hard to see anything with the mixture of blackened furniture and ash all around him. Even the sheriff didn't really know what he was looking for. He had never had to deal with an event such as this, and truth be told, he was afraid he wouldn't be able to figure out what happened or who did it. After a few loops around the interior of the saloon, the sheriff decided there was nothing there that could help them.

"Let's go to the church," he said. "Maybe we'll have better luck there."

"Sheriff!"

They were walking toward the church when Dwain came running to them.

"Sheriff, I've got something for you," he said as he came to a stop in front of them and handed the sheriff a piece of blackened paper. "I found it in the pastor's coat pocket," Dwain explained.

The sheriff looked at the paper. "Thanks, Dwain," he said. "I'll take a look at this when I get back to the jail."

Dwain nodded and walked off.

The sheriff stood there, playing with the paper for a moment longer.

"What is it?" Henry asked.

"I'm not quite sure. It looks like it might be a note." The sheriff folded up the paper and stuck it in his front shirt pocket. "Let's get on down to the church and see if we find something there," he said.

They were almost to the church when they were stopped again.

"Sheriff! Henry!" Both men turned at the sound of Lucy's voice. Henry walked quickly over to her, the sheriff following.

"What is it, Lucy?" the sheriff asked.

"Mark is in there." She pointed at the DeWitts' house. "He's holding the DeWitts, Matthew, and Ms. Betty at gunpoint. I snuckout when we all got up from the table so Matthew could dig a bullet out of him."

Henry moved to go into the house, but the sheriff stopped him. "I think it would be better if I went in by myself," he told Henry.

Henry nodded in agreement and stayed put. When the sheriff had gone inside, Henry took a long look at Lucy, cupped his hand under her chin, and tilted her face up toward his.

"Are you alright?" he asked.

Lucy placed her hand on top of his. "Yes," she said.

Henry dropped his hand and pulled her to him, hugging her tightly against his chest. Lucy relaxed into his embrace, letting go of the tension she had felt since Mark had come into the DeWitts' home.

&

Chapter Thirty-Two

A pistol cocked behind them. Henry turned toward the sound, pulling Lucy behind his back.

"Hello there, little brother," Sam said.

"How did you get out of the jail, Sam?" Henry asked.

"Dwain came by looking for the sheriff," Sam said. "He was kind enough to let me out."

Henry remembered how Dwain had seemed nervous when they saw him earlier.

"What do you want, Sam?"

"Well, how about we go—"

"Daddy!" Sammy squealed as he came running from the wagon that had pulled up beside them. "Daddy, what are you doing? Why are you pointing a gun at Uncle Henry?"

"Sammy, come here," Beth called from beside Henry and Lucy.

"What are you doing here?" Sam asked, ignoring his son's question and keeping the gun on Henry.

"I decided to come see why neither of you had come back to the ranch yet," Beth explained.

"You shouldn't have brought the boy," Sam scolded.

"He's not old enough to leave out there alone," Beth said, her tone just as sharp. "Besides, he needs to see how his daddy really is."

Sam could feel his face getting hot. "Let's all go inside, shall we," he said, swinging the gun toward the house and forcing all of them to turn and walk in front of him.

❧

Blood from Mark's wound continued to saturate his shirt. Matthew said he had gotten the bullet out, but Lucy wondered if that was true. He had packed the area with one of Mrs. DeWitt's towels he had ripped up, but that hadn't seemed to stop the bleeding.

They were all crowded around the DeWitts' table. Sammy sat in a chair beside Mark, wide-eyed and watching his dad.

For all the strength she tried her best to have, Lucy was frightened. The two men who were the most capable of evil were before her. She knew they were responsible for yesterday's events.

Henry was watching Sam pacing with the gun. Lucy glanced at Henry's side and noticed, for the first time, that he also carried a gun. "Has it been there every time I've seen him?" she wondered.

"Sam, you should let Beth and Sammy go home," Henry said.

Sam walked over to Henry and aimed his gun in his little brother's face. "Why don't you stay quiet, little brother?" he said.

"Sam," Beth pleaded, "do you really want your son to see you like this?"

"What's so wrong with me?" Sam asked, waving his gun around. "All my life, I never could measure up to anyone's standards, especially with my little brother around."

Sam spun around and cocked the gun in Henry's face once more. This time, Henry anticipated it and mirrored his brother's actions.

"You're a fool, Sam," Henry said, "a no-good fool."

"Why's that, Henry?" Sam asked. "Just because I like to have a good time?"

"Anyone can have a good time, Sam," Henry said, "but you seem to always hurt someone while doing it."

Sam cocked his gun again. "Not true!" Sam shouted.

The sheriff finally spoke up. "Boys, this isn't the place to air out your family troubles."

Henry looked at the sheriff, then back at Sam before he released the trigger and put his gun back in the holster. "You're not worth the bullet," he said to Sam.

"Yeah, well you are," Sam said.

"No!"

Everyone jumped when Mrs. DeWitt shouted.

She stepped in front of Henry and faced Sam. "You want to kill your brother, you do it outside this house," Mrs. DeWitt said.

Sheriff Daniel used Mrs. DeWitt's distraction to take Sam's gun away, place his hands behind his back, and put handcuffs on him.

"It was you!" Mrs. DeWitt said. "You and Mark came into the store while I was helping the pastor. One of you hit me with something and I passed out."

"That would be me," Mark said from the center of the room, his right hand holding his wound and his left holding a gun.

"Where did you get the gun?" the sheriff asked.

"Matthew shouldn't be so careless when he's helping people," Mark said, turning to face Mrs. DeWitt. "If I had my way, you would actually be dead, but Sam here wouldn't hear of it." Mark looked at Henry. "Surprising, huh, Henry? Your brother isn't as bad as you thought after all."

Mark started pacing, making circles around the sheriff, Sam, and Mrs. DeWitt. "You see," Mark started again, "Sam isn't all that evil. He just enjoys a good time and should have never gotten married." Mark stopped in front of Sam. "Well, there was that one." Mark looked at Beth. "Your husband killed some man in California because he couldn't pay his debt to him."

Beth had moved over to Sammy, who was now crying into her shoulder. "That's enough, Mark," she said.

"No, I don't think so, Beth." Mark continued to pace, stopping in front of Lucy and tapping the gun against his leg.

Henry put his arm around Lucy. "Leave her alone, Mark," he said.

"No, Henry." Mark stepped closer to Lucy. "She's the reason we're all here today." He turned to Mrs. DeWitt. "Isn't that right, Mrs. DeWitt?"

❧

Chapter Thirty-Three

Mrs. DeWitt was speechless.

"Oh, come now," Mark said. "You always have something to say. Now isn't the time to be quiet." Mark nonchalantly aimed the gun toward Mr. DeWitt. "Tell the truth or your husband dies, or do you care what happens to him?"

Mrs. DeWitt pursed her lips for a moment and finally spoke. "Yes, it's true."

"What?" Ms. Betty said. "What are you saying?"

"Lucy came to me months ago and demanded I get her a job at the store. Without her, though, I wouldn't have known I have a stepson."

Mark burst out laughing. "Oh, Lucy, I didn't know you had it in you to be so rotten," he said, looking back at Mrs. DeWitt. "So now you know Wyatt is Mr. DeWitt's son. Where is the little rascal anyway?" Mark asked, turning to face Ms. Betty.

"He's with one of the girls."

"Oh well, too bad he can't join us." Mark continued pacing and stopped in front of Lucy. "Back to what I was saying. You should have never come to check on Melissa. Everything was just fine until you did that," he said, pointing the gun in Lucy's face. "I beat it out of her the very night you told her."

Lucy jerked forward, but Henry stopped her. "Leave her alone, Mark," Henry said.

"Ah, yes, the ever-dutiful good brother." Mark moved his aim to Henry's face. "You know, that's how I got Sam on board. When you decided to stick around for a while, I decided to send your brother a telegram informing him of all the wonderful things you were doing with his wife. I knew he hated you, and I counted on that to help me get back at Lucy."

Mark lowered his gun and paced again. Lucy felt Henry move his hand to his own gun.

"I started keeping my eye on you, Lucy, trying to figure out what you were planning. I suspect you didn't really know yourself." Mark stopped. "But then Mrs. DeWitt did as you asked, and for some reason, you seemed to stop being so vengeful. Not sure I understand what happened there." He began to pace again. "So, maybe those plans of yours changed?" He stopped and looked at her. "But mine hadn't." He smiled coldly at her. "No, I couldn't chance you getting into Melissa's head and having her do something stupid like leaving me. She's the perfect little maid, you know." He waved his gun at her. "No, we had to move forward, Sam and me." He looked at Matthew. "Should have never told us we weren't welcome there. You weren't part of the plan until you did that."

"You son of a bitch!" Matthew lashed out at him.

"No!" Ms. Betty screamed as the gunshot shattered the shock-filled room.

Matthew was on the floor, bleeding from his arm. Ms. Betty knelt down to help him.

"I thought you were smarter than that, Matthew," Mark said, waving his gun at him and beginning to pace again. "Now, back to what I was saying. Yes, Mrs. DeWitt, it was me that hit you. You see, we needed kerosene to start the fires, so we used the good ole pastor to get into your store." Mark turned back to Lucy. "Only, the pastor wasn't so good, was he, Lucy?"

Lucy stayed silent, and Mark laughed and began pacing again.

"Our good pastor frequented the upstairs of the saloon," Mark continued and stopped pacing. "I think Catherine was his favorite." As he began to pace again, he said, "We couldn't let Pastor Tom live after he helped us, so I made him go to the church with us. I shot him and left him to die in the fire."

"Why?" Mrs. DeWitt asked.

Mark looked at her. "Because you all deserve it for looking down your noses at us. You're no better than us. Lucy was at least smart enough to see that, but that doesn't make her innocent in this. If she hadn't decided to share with Melissa that she had a plan against me, I don't know that I would have done any of this."

Mark went and stood at the window and turned to face everyone.

"I hadn't planned on setting a third fire, but I think this has all come about nicely." He dug a match out of his pocket, walked over to the table, took the top off the kerosene lamp, and dipped a piece of rag into the liquid. Holding it up, he said, "Any last words?"

Chapter Thirty-Four

The window shattered as he was about to strike the match. Mark had a surprised look on his face as he fell forward, bleeding from his chest.

Lucy broke from Henry and ran to the window. "Melissa!" she shouted.

Melissa ran around the corner to the front of the house and into the kitchen, carrying a shotgun. "Is he dead?' she asked.

Henry walked over to Melissa and eased the shotgun away from her. Lucy stood in front of her and took her hands. They were shaking.

"Melissa," Lucy said, "what are you doing here?"

Melissa kept her eyes glued on Mark. "I'm condemning him to hell!" she yelled.

"She's in shock," Mrs. DeWitt said as she took Melissa gently by the shoulders and led her to a chair. "Get her some water, Lucy."

Lucy did as she was told and sat down across from her best friend.

"Is he dead?" Melissa asked again.

"Yes, dear," Mrs. DeWitt said, "he's dead."

"Good," Melissa said. She took a deep breath, and in an instant, tears flowed down her face. "He was an evil man," she said between sobs. "It looked like he was going to kill you."

"Melissa, how did you know to come here?" Sheriff Daniel asked, kneeling before her.

Melissa took a minute and stared at the sheriff. "He hadn't come home," she said. "I could feel something wasn't right. It was a strong feeling, like nothing I'd ever felt before. I just had to come, especially after all the smoke I could see yesterday."

"Well, I'm glad you followed your gut," the sheriff said softly, standing up to face Sam. "You're under arrest, Sam. Let's go," he said, putting his hand in the crook of Sam's arm as they walked out the door.

"Daddy!" Sammy yelled.

Henry knelt down in front of his nephew. "Your dad is going to be gone for a while again, Sammy," he told him.

"Is my dad a bad man, Uncle Henry?"

Henry took a minute. "Sammy, the truth is that your dad has some confused ideas and because of that, he makes bad decisions."

"Will he get better?" Sammy asked.

"I don't know," Henry said as he stood up.

"Let's go home, Sammy," Beth said. She looked at Henry. "We'll see you later?" she asked. "Maybe you could bring Lucy out for supper."

Henry smiled a sheepish smile. "Thanks, Beth."

❧

Ms. Betty helped Matthew up. She had managed to get a rag tied around his arm. As they walked out, she stopped in front of Mrs. DeWitt and said, "I'll be glad to bring Wyatt by anytime."

Mrs. DeWitt smiled. "I'd like that. Thank you."

It was just the DeWitts, Henry, Lucy, and Melissa left in the kitchen.

"Well, why don't we clean this place up?" Mrs. DeWitt suggested.

Everyone started picking up glass, sweeping, and wiping away blood.

Melissa tried to get up and help.

"No, Melissa," Mrs. DeWitt said. "You stay put. You did quite enough helping all of us out of a very bad situation."

❧

Chapter Thirty-Five

An hour later, Henry and Lucy stood awkwardly with each other on the DeWitts' porch.

"Are you going back to Beth's place?" Lucy asked, breaking the silence.

"Yeah," Henry said. "I need to finish a few things up there and get back to Charlotte."

Lucy's back went rigid. "Charlotte?"

Henry reached out, pulled her to him, and looked down into her eyes, glancing quickly at her scar. Her body remained stiff in his arms.

"Lucy," he said in barely a whisper.

Before she could respond, he kissed her. Lucy could feel the tension release in her body. She tried to fight it, but the kiss she had waited so long for was melting it away.

When he released her, he placed his hand under her chin and lifted her face to meet his gaze. "Lucy, Charlotte is my daughter. My wife died giving birth to her. My parents have been taking care of her since I came here. I need to get back to her."

Lucy slumped her head onto his shoulder and began to cry softly.

He lifted her head again and said, "Lucy, I want you to go back with me. I'm in love with you."

"I love you, too," Lucy said between sobs, "but I don't know if I can go."

"Why not? What's holding you here?" he asked.

"Nothing," she admitted. "I don't know. I just don't know, Henry."

"It'll be a few days still before I leave. That'll give you some time to think on it." He released her from his embrace and kissed her again. "I hope you decide to go with me," he said as he turned and walked away.

Lucy stood there, looking after him, wondering why she didn't just say yes then.

"Everything okay, dear?"

Lucy turned to see Mrs. DeWitt coming out the front door. "Oh, Mrs. DeWitt," she said between sobs, "I've made a mess of everything."

Mrs. DeWitt put her arms around Lucy. "Now, what makes you say that?" she asked.

"I just wanted Mark to stop hurting Melissa, and I was so mad at everyone for not helping her," Lucy rambled. "I never meant for people to get hurt or die." Lucy's body shook as she started to cry harder. "I didn't mean it, I didn't," she said.

Mrs. DeWitt pulled back from her, keeping her hands on Lucy's shoulders.

"Lucy, you can't blame yourself for everything that happened," Mrs. DeWitt said, "and shame on us for not helping Melissa, but it wasn't a problem for you to solve, no matter how much you wanted to help her."

Lucy took a breath. "I just couldn't stand the way he treated her."

"I know, Lucy. It's over now."

"No, it isn't," Lucy replied.

"What do you mean?" Mrs. DeWitt asked.

"I've hurt people here—you and Mr. DeWitt," Lucy said. "And Matthew is without a business. I'm a part of all that," Lucy said.

"What are you saying, Lucy?"

"I think it's best if I leave. There's too much pain here," she said.

"Where will you go?"

"I don't know. Henry wants me to go back with him, but I don't know if that's the right thing to do."

"Lucy," Mrs. DeWitt said, after being silent for a moment, "do you love Henry?"

"Yes, I think so."

"Then go with him," Mrs. DeWitt said. "Don't misunderstand me. I want you to stay. I've grown to love you like a daughter, but Lucy, he loves you. Go with him. Give yourself a new chance at life."

"What about Melissa?" Lucy asked.

"Melissa will be fine. She's got more strength than even she realizes. Besides, I'll make sure she's okay. I won't neglect her, I promise."

Lucy started crying again. "Oh, Mrs. DeWitt, I just don't know. I'm scared," she finally admitted.

"Scared of what, Lucy?"

"Scared his love is just a dream. I know that's silly, but no man ever wanted or loved me before."

"Lucy," Mrs. DeWitt said softly, "that's because the right man hadn't fallen in love with you before."

Be on the lookout for more details regarding release of Book 2 in the *Colorado Reckoning Western Series.*